LAST OLD BEAR

A NOVEL BY

J. ARTHUR EIDSON

© 2015

James A. Eidson

Dedication

Dedicated to my love, Anita, and with gratitude for the help of Niki McDaniel, Diana Stokely, and all friends and relatives who read and provided expertise and moral support. This book is further dedicated to the old settlers, and the old tradition of storytelling.

All persons depicted in this book are fictitious. Resemblance to persons living or dead is coincidental.

Contents

BOOK 1

CHAPTER 1

"Looky here." Uncle Gus slowly opened his hand. Inside, there was a small horned lizard, which Gus called a horny toad. Gus had pulled it from the limestone wall at the back of the house. The wall loomed high above young Sam Wood's head as he peered into Gus's hand. The rows of stacked stone served to display all of the natural bric-a-brac that Aunt Mabel had collected in the last thirty-five years. Quartz crystals as big as a cat's head, arrowheads, geodes, various broken pieces of farm implements from the long-passed old settlers were arranged along the stair-stepped stonework. In the middle of the long wall, a cellar was dug into the hillside. The cellar was sometimes the family's place of refuge during tornado weather, but usually it was just a place for rattlesnakes and bad bugs to take refuge from the heat.

July 10, 1912, was a hot day. No sound, other than the buzzing of a few cicadas, was heard in the afternoon heat. It was common for most of the central Texas town of Hamilton to doze on a sweltering July afternoon. Sam and his Uncle Gus were the only ones moving among the houses along Rice Street. Uncle Gus gently placed the lizard into the boy's hand.

"Now you be gentle with him, or he'll squirt blood from his eyes," he said. "And you might stain your shirt." Gus grinned and watched the lizard wiggle in Sam's hand.

1

Aunt Mabel was particular about how boys kept their shirts. His had been starched and ironed that very morning. Aunt Mabel was the most erect person Sam had ever seen. Her posture had been the subject of conjecture among certain Hamiltonians who did not share her gift for erectness. When Mabel moved from room to room, tending to her chores, the top of her head neither rose nor fell more than one-quarter of an inch. This effect, along with feet hidden by her long skirt, gave Sam the impression that she floated. This lent her a rather spectral appearance, and enhanced his suspicion that the collection on her sandstone wall might be more magical than decorative.

Sam held the horny toad, which neither bled from his eyes nor tried to escape. His finger traced the spiny backbone of the lizard, and felt the two horns which rose from his brow in such a way that he was reminded of a tiny, flattened buffalo. Uncle Gus had told him about the days when there were many buffalo on the prairies surrounding the town, which had been a settlement of tents and a few clapboard buildings at the time. Except for the town square and the adjoining neighborhood, the prairie was much as it had always been: yellow and silent; billowing in the wind like waves on the sea. The buffalo and the Comanches were gone. Not so gone that they were forgotten by those who lived through the closing of the frontier. Uncle Gus was one of those, and, sometimes, if Sam asked, he would answer questions about the old days, and occasionally tell long and wonderful stories. Though he had no real sense of Gus's age, he thought Gus was ancient.

By the time supper was ready, Sam had soiled his shirt, but the day was done, and stains would not show so much in the dimmer light, he thought. Aunt Mabel had made a coarse supper of boiled potatoes and canned beef. In years past, servants had tended to the cooking and chores she now assumed. That was before Judge Edwards, her husband, had passed, and though the house was large and the appointments elegant, the Judge had been less than judicious in his investments. Mabel was not quite destitute, though dangerously close. Her bachelor brother, Gus Wheelis, had moved in soon after the Judge's death to share expenses and tend the various chores the house and grounds demanded. After a vigorous whisking by Aunt Mabel, Sam and Gus seated themselves at the table, which was overly long and overly empty. A very small crystal salt cellar at the center of the table was provided, Sam thought, for scale, much the same way one might pose a person next to the edge of a big empty canyon for a photograph. Uncle Gus was required to wear, at least, his waistcoat and tie, and young Sam his topcoat. It did not seem to matter that Gus's pants were frayed or that Sam was barefoot. It was the portion that poked above the table that mattered. Grace was offered, and the food was consumed in silence.

Dusk was only slightly cooler than the middle of the day. The leaves of the China tree in front of the house had wilted and its porcelain berries lay scattered beneath its canopy, lending the air the scent of fermenting fruit along with the usual summer smell of dust. Sam sat in a rocking chair on the long front porch and breathed in the coming night. It seemed to Sam that he could smell fall coming. He thought it might only be wishful thinking, because Gus said it might only be the smell of drought-stricken and dying vegetation. He had sat on this porch nightly —with the exception of times of coldest weather and during the two weeks he had had

3

pneumonia— since he came to live with Gus and Mabel two years before. He had been ten years old.

Sam, his mother and father, and younger sister had lived on a farm on the Leon River bottomlands, about ten miles from Hamilton. It had been a relatively prosperous cotton farm, with pigs and an orchard of young pecan trees. When Sam was five, both mother and sister were stricken with typhoid. Though a cabal of aunts and great aunts ministered the sick ones, both were dead within a few days of becoming ill. His father, Abbott Wood, had turned him over to his sister-in-law, and left for the southeast Texas oil fields. Since then, Sam had passed from one household to the next, competing with his array of cousins for affection, justice, and, most importantly, food. Sam had always been small, and found his short arms and little fingers poorly adapted to seize food from the table before his taller and longer cousins got it first. The boy's Aunt Melba (one of the many variations in name which also included two Maybelles and a Malba), last of the line of Aunts, reluctantly took Sam in, and when the family's cotton crop failed during the drought of 1910, she could no longer keep him fed.

One day, Aunt Melba rousted Sam from bed at an early hour. She was dressed for travel and had a sad look, and patted his hair so much he looked like his head was flat on top. It took almost a day to reach Hamilton, and though she did not have much to say on the trip, it was clear he was to be relocated to the next aunt — Great Aunt Mabel. Aunt Melba accompanied him into a long foyer they called the reception hall. To the left, behind paneled pocket doors, was the parlor, and to the right was the less formal sitting room, which was filled with cigar boxes of arrowheads, quartz crystals, a stereopticon and in short, everything that could distract a boy. He was received by Aunt Mabel, however, in the parlor. Aunt Mabel was seated at the edge of a straight backed chair, while Melba and Sam sat on the edge of a small, worn, love seat. The room was otherwise empty except for a piano, a clock, and some photographs in oval frames, hung from long wires which seemed attached near the distant ceiling. Sam could tell from the protracted silence, interrupted only by the ticking clock on the piano, that his great Aunt was mentally preparing a foreword to a long, book-sized speech. Mabel fidgeted with a lace handkerchief which usually hung at her waist. This was how Aunt Mabel's speech began:

"Our family (she pronounced our as "owa") —your mother's family— is one of note, Samuel. Our history in South Carolina goes back to before the Revolutionary War. Your great-great grandmother was a descendant of the Hapsburgs, though I would not expect a youngster to know of that illustrious history. The family was one of the first to settle Texas, and came long before that hill riff-raff from Tennessee. Therefore, it is incumbent on you to hold up the family's name and honor. Reputation is our prized possession, Samuel, and it will not be surrendered without a struggle ..."

Mabel went on to specify Sam's position in the household, daily chores, the wearing of clean shirts on a daily basis, cleanliness of noses; etiquette concerning both Mabel's elderly lady guests and meals; and above all, permissible noises (none). As the speech droned on, Sam noted the water stains on the ceiling paper. They made large brown and rust clouds which sailed across a beige paper sky. A fly, caught between the window glass and the window screen, buzzed. An itch between Samuel's fingers was scratched.

After a long time, Mabel concluded, caught her breath, and asked,

"Are we clear, Samuel?"

"Yas'm," responded Sam.

He was assigned a small bedroom on the second floor. The upstairs consisted of a central stairway, and a large U-shaped landing with four bedrooms arranged along the arms of the U. At the end of the left arm, a small door opened to the attic. Sam's room was next to this door. Sam placed his few articles of clothing on hooks inside the armoire. There was a bed with a dusty coverlet and a small table next to it. A glass of water sat on the table. A fly floated there. A window opened to the widow's walk facing Rice Street. As he stood watching the dust motes illumined by the window, Uncle Gus entered the room and cleared his throat.

"Boy?" called Gus. "I want to show you something."

He motioned for Sam to follow him. Gus opened the little attic door. There were four high steps set at an oblique angle to the wall. Gus and Sam stepped up. In the attic, four dormers looked upon the courthouse at the center of the town square, to the prairie beyond and to the low hills beyond the prairie.

"Sam, that courthouse is where your great uncle, Judge Edwards, presided for over 20 years. He saw the courthouse burn down twice. He was lucky he wasn't in it.

If you look to the range just beyond town? That is where Old Man Rufus Stewart and his two boys were ambushed by the Comanches and killed in '56. It was a sad time. Mr. Stewart was pastor of a little church that had fifteen members and a pump organ. I recall that he had a large brown wart on the left side of his nose, which I suppose kept the congregation's attention fixed more than his sermons did. Beyond that — do you see where the trees get heavy out in the mid-distance? That is the Leon River bottom where Anne Whitney had her school. Miss Whitney was killed by the Comanches, but managed to save her students. She pushed them under the floorboards and squeezed them out the window, but she was too fat to fit either of them. And way out on the horizon — can you see two mountains that stand together, and look alike? That's Twin Mountains. They are all the way over near the town of Fairy, more than 20 miles away. We will get over there later in the summer. There is a man I have to see, and his wife always has pie."

Two summers passed, and Sam had yet to sample the pie of the wife of the man in Fairy.

The morning of July 12, was hot with a steady wind from the southwest that promised to bring even more heat. Gus found Sam at the back of the house cutting the grass at the base of the wall with an old kitchen knife.

"Boy?" Gus called from the corner of the house. "Let's have us some fun."

He followed Uncle Gus into a little servant's quarters behind the kitchen, where Gus had laid out some newspaper. Gus looked down at Sam. He chuckled.

"You ever worn a paper hat?"

Sam had not had much of any hat, ever. Gus folded and folded again, until he had made a triangular hat which he placed on Sam's head. He had seen the younger boys playing soldier with hats such as this, and was mortified that Gus would think of him as "little" enough to play dress-up. Gus gestured grandly toward the house.

"Now ... Go stand inside the front door just at the bottom of the stairs, and leave the door open."

Sam positioned himself as Gus had directed. Gus rushed up the stairs, and after a bit, Sam could hear Gus opening all of the windows in the upstairs rooms. As he did so, the breeze through the front door increased incrementally with the opening of each window. Finally, Sam heard Gus's footsteps on the attic stairs, and then heard him opening the dormer windows. Suddenly, Sam's pant legs flapped and the paper hat sailed off of his head and began a slow and wobbling progress up the stairs, suspended in air as if it was worn by a disembodied and tipsy spirit intent on getting off to bed. As the hat disappeared into the upstairs shadows, Sam fell on the floor and laughed so hard that snot came out of his nose.

By the time Gus came downstairs, Sam had regained some of his composure, but he still wiped tears from his eyes. Gus had brought with him an armful of feathers, several of Aunt Mabel's old hats (Aunt Mabel being at the market at the time), various papers and a silk scarf or two. They spent the remainder of the morning launching these articles of Mabel's wardrobe and library up the stairs. The lighter pieces made it all of the way to the attic where they were held fast to the window screens. For several nights following, Sam lay awake considering all of the possible practical applications of the phenomenon.

CHAPTER 2

Aunt Mabel's house was close to downtown, and Sam spent much time wandering the square. A courthouse, the second in what would become a sequence of three, stood as a demonstration of the imposing architecture public will and bonds could manifest. Mansard roofs graced two towers of limestone, while young pecan trees and trampled grass made up its lawn. Seasonally dusty or muddy streets surrounded the courthouse. The square was the city's mercantile district. It was made of limestone and milled planks. New construction and use made the square smell like fresh lumber and horse manure. The stores were fronted by boardwalks which lifted the pedestrians a few feet above the street and which provided the various dogs and smaller boys refuge from heat, bullies, and mothers bent on placing the former in new, stiff, clothes. Sam liked to climb under the walks and eavesdrop on the conversations of those above. They pertained mostly to the weather and crops and cattle. Occasionally, however, gossip about misbehavior made dodging the dribble of tobacco juice worthwhile. He was forbidden from loitering on the north side of the square, however. Like most central Texas towns of any merit, Hamilton supported no less than six saloons, all relegated to the one side. They had alluring names, like the Silver Dollar, the Basement, and the Watson. The latter was preferred by Gus and the other older and established gentlemen of the community — those who were referred to by the younger as "old man" so and so. The designation did not necessarily reflect age as much as having membership within the establishment. The Watson Saloon was elegantly appointed with a mahogany bar and brass rail, backed by a mirror and row upon row of shiny bottles; spittoons which were emptied and polished on a regular basis; and ten fine oak tables with matching chairs — not one broken or wobbly. Even a tab from the Watson sported its name in elegant script arranged around the rendering of a stag's head. In short, compared to the Basement and a few others of livelier reputation, the Watson maintained an uncommon atmosphere of civility. Men of substance or age gathered to discuss business and politics, and whereas these same topics might result in fisticuffs in lesser establishments, the alcohol, combined with the gentility of its clientele, served to induce a groggy and early retreat to beds occupied by stern, but usually silent, wives.

In the evening, following supper, the three often retired to the sitting room: Aunt Mabel doing handwork; Sam examining the contents of various boxes; and Gus smoking and fidgeting until he announced he would take the air. This announcement was never acknowledged by Aunt Mabel, and the room would suddenly become quieter than it should have. This was always followed by Mabel's suggestion that it was time for Sam to retire for the night. On one such evening Sam overheard Uncle Gus's return. Sam could hear his unsteady gait on the stair. Aunt Mabel stood at the foot of the stairway and observed, "What a fine specimen you are!" After due consideration, Uncle Gus responded, "Mabel, you may think of me what you want, but please don't call me a specimen." Aunt Mabel was not only opposed to Gus's drinking, but drinking in general. She was the chairwoman of the local chapter of the Women's Christian Temperance Movement. This position made Gus's drinking all the more intolerable.

On the heels of this conflict, Mabel received a telegram that state chapter president, the Reverend Mr. Elbert Dellwood, was coming to visit the WCTM chapter in Hamilton to "magnify the Chapter's clarion call to all clear headed Texans" and that he would "mount the pulpit with the sword of temperance in hand."

"It just means he's going to be loud," said Gus upon reading the telegram.

Aunt Mabel's excitement over being chosen for the honor was infectious, though support for the cause which elicited it was not. For Gus and Sam, the weeks leading up to the Reverend's visit consisted of daily meetings with Mabel at the kitchen table which resulted in long lists of chores, and admonitions concerning Sam's and Gus's comportment. She suggested that they rehearse the latter before the appointed day.

Three weeks of preparation were interrupted by the visitation, in groups and singly, of members of WCTM. These were what Gus referred to as Mabel's "elderly lady friends," though to Sam they seemed no more worn than Mabel or Gus. The ladies arrived unannounced, there being no telephone at the Edwards' residence, and their issues pressing to the extent that appropriate calling cards or mailed notes were inopportune. The condition of being open to surprise inspection placed Mabel on high alert, caused Sam to change a week's worth of shirts in a day, and drove Gus to the refuge of the Watson saloon with greater frequency and at earlier hours than was usually his habit. At long last, the Rev. Dellwood arrived on the Waco train. Mabel had arranged for the train to be met by the town band, consisting of two bugles, a fife, a tuba and snare drum. The band was composed of men having sufficient time on their hands to learn their instruments, meaning that these represented the old, or infirm. In general, those men only capable of producing a thin and reedy rendition of the two or three pieces of appropriately martial or religious music they knew.

Rev. Albert Ross, pastor of the Methodist Church, delivered the welcome and invocation. Rev. Dellwood was expected to deliver Sunday's sermon, but for the time being, refreshments for the candidate and the WCTM were to be served at Mabel's house. Sam and Gus waited for their arrival in their best clothing, usually reserved for church and funerals.

"Sam, I believe it is a bit close in here," said Gus. "I think you should open the upstairs windows, to draw a bit of breeze through. If that don't freshen it, perhaps you could open the attic windows at the appropriate time. As a matter of business, I think it would be good of you to station yourself in the attic to await my signal."

Rev. Dellwood and his entourage arrived in three carriages and one automobile, driven by Rev. Ross. Gus opened the door, and called to Sam just as Dellwood and the first of the WCTM entered the foyer. The first indication of trouble was the erratic movement of the egret and peacock feathers on two of the more massive and fashionable hats. These had sufficient weight and hat pins to do little more than flutter. However, several seasonably lightweight hats began a stately procession up the stairs, along with Rev. Dellwood's boater. The sudden breeze had been interpreted as merely that, though Mabel surreptitiously pinched Gus so hard he flinched. Hats were retrieved, refreshments were served, and Dellwood taken to the home of the pastor, it being unseemly for him to stay in the household of an unmarried woman.

CHAPTER 3

In early August, the day arrived for Gus's business with the man in Fairy. Sam did not inquire about Gus's business nor did Gus offer. However, he looked forward to a long ride on the range with Gus, and the prospect of pie at the end of the trail was particularly attractive. Gus and Mabel did not own a horse, but instead had a mule which was pastured behind the house and rarely ridden. Gus could not afford to hire a horse from the livery on the town square, but had borrowed an old nag belonging to a neighbor. The horse had a misshapen jaw, probably brought on by mashing her nose too close to the twitching hindquarters of the horse ahead of her.

The open range had come to an end long before Sam was born. Barbed wire, referred to by some old men as "the Devil's hat band" became readily available thirty years prior. The first rolls of wire had featured nasty barbs which had ruined some cattle, though it effectively contained them. The range had been diced up into small pieces, though a number of ranches still contained tens of thousands of acres. The Rocking B Ranch is one of these. It had begun as five sections but, by the late 1880's, had begun to consume surrounding small holders so that by the turn of the century the ranch laid claim to 50,000 acres. A great drought in 1886 had coincided with the fencing of the land, and as the grass perished under confined grazing, so perished the small holder. The founder of the Rocking B, Chapman Bilch, had come to Texas from Georgia, seeking his fortune in the field of land speculation and cattle. As his fortunes waxed, those of his neighbors waned. The ranch passed to his only son,

Ruder Bilch. Ruder was as jealous of his wealth and holdings as had been his father.

The south-most fence of the Rocking B stretched for miles and obstructed the road to Fairy. However, community lanes criss-crossed the landscape and many private holdings were by custom, if not by law, accessible to the public. A gap in the fence, outfitted with five strands of loose wire and a tie post was provided to the public. There had been several disputes between Bilch and the town, the most recent when several dozen cattle grazed the courthouse lawn and fouled the streets. Though the community lane gate had obviously been maliciously left open, local sentiment held with the offender, rather than the offended. Offended he was, and his effort to patrol and enclose his land was redoubled.

Sam and Gus had some difficulty with the neighbor's horse who tried to bite Sam each time he attempted to mount. Gus cheeked the animal, pulling the reins so that her head was flush with her right flank. Once Sam had mounted, however, she surrendered and proved to be a reasonable though somewhat dejected mount. Finally, they departed the horse lot. Sam had never had such a sense of adventure and importance. They rode north on Rice Street and on through the square. Sam peeked from the corner of his eye to see if he had attracted admiring or even envious looks from those poor un-mounted boys on the street. All of this grandeur ended just outside of town when Gus could not get the wire off of the tie post to open the gate. Bilch, following the recent event of the escaped cattle, had become determined to make it damnably inconvenient to open the gate. Gus had never used profanity in front of Sam, but he heard several mutterings having the requisite cadence and emphasis.

Gus's face reddened, and he untied his saddle bag and retrieved a pair of wire cutters.

"Since he don't appear to want traffic through *this* gate, I reckon I'll make him a new one." he hissed.

Sam was shocked and little afraid. Cutting fence was once an offense that could get one killed and even in these more modern times, might be considered breaking the law. Gus quickly cut the five strands next to the gate, tied them tight to the next post in line and made a gate post out of an old discarded cedar line post. Gus sucked his teeth and admired his work.

"That should suit the most discriminating." In fact, it was as serviceable and well-constructed as the old one had been.

The range north of the fence was in far better condition than the smaller places close to town. Bluestem grasses, Indiangrass and switchgrass cloaked the slopes and bottoms. A carpet of russet and blue-green stretched to the horizon. Even though the country had suffered several years of drought, the grasses still swept the bottoms of their stirrups. Grasshoppers sang in the grass, and flew by the hundreds as they parted it. On the hilltops, bare limestone stood out white as clouds. Hardy weeds emerged from the fractures in the rocks, and deep ledges provided shade for the abundant rattlesnakes. Gus and Sam stopped for a moment to admire the view. Gus shook his head.

"Sometimes I forget what this country was like. It seems like ever year there're more houses and barns, and more brush and more plowed land. But, this ... this is what it was, Sam. Bluestem range as far as you can point your hand. It

19

was dangerous country, though. I reckon I don't miss that feature of it."

They rode on in silence. White cumulus clouds passed overhead in the hot breeze and their shadows made a cool spot that raced from valley to hillside and beyond. Sam tried to keep up with them to stay in the shade. He noticed a level area pock-marked with shallow basins. Sam pointed them out to Gus, who replied that they were old buffalo wallows, and they would be worth investigating. The visible wallows were less than one-half mile away, but Sam noticed the abundance of uneven ground they rode through. Small and large wallows, many hidden by the luxurious grasses, covered a hundred acres or more. Gus dismounted and knelt by a wallow. He pulled up some soil and sniffed it.

"They say that buffalo visited these wallows every year, both on their trip south in the fall and then again in the spring when they were headed north. One old man told me that he reckoned they had been doin' the same for hundreds of years."

Sam saw a small glint of white near the edge of one of the wallows. It was a buffalo horn. Sam brushed the soil away, and with some effort, pulled up a buffalo skull. Sam was amazed at its size.

"That come from an old bull," said Gus. He was excited. "I guess he was mighty old and mighty big. I remember the herd. When I was a child, the sound of them running woke me up at night more than once. The sound was like a big wind, or a long roll of thunder. They seemed to always come through the saddle of a couple of camel-backed hills on the south side of the county. I saw that big herd once, in daylight, and it started on the south horizon and nearly made it to the north. I wish you could'a seen it." Sam wished he had seen it, too. They rode on.

"This country had more life in it than you could shake a stick at," Gus wiped the sweat from his hatband with a red bandana. "In those days, we might not have seen buffalo, but we surely would have seen pronghorns and deer, maybe buffalo wolves, too. It seemed like once the Comanches had been whupped, all the rest of it got whupped too."

Sam saw a little flash of blue and green and spurred his horse into a trot. A largish lizard, a "mountain boomer" had caught his eye. If these had become scarcer it was because small boys had tormented them out of existence. He dismounted and ran after the lizard, which was running full tilt on his hind legs, with his front legs curled under his chin. He disappeared beneath a ledge of limestone. Sam scrambled up the slope to the ledge and thrust his hand under.

Sam screamed as he recoiled from the buzzing, three- foot diamond-back rattlesnake attached to his right hand. Gus had been following Sam at a walk, but spurred the mule to a gallop. By the time he reached Sam, the snake had released his hand and had made it back under the ledge. The skin around the bite had already taken on ominous purple and brown hues. Gus knelt beside him.

"Boy, we got to get you on in to Fairy and find a doctor. I don't have much to treat you with other than a little coal oil and a rag. That'll have to do for the time bein'."

Sam looked in disbelief at his swelling hand. He began to taste something unpleasant and metallic at the back of his throat. He pitched forward and vomited. After Gus treated the bite, he helped Sam into the saddle.

"We want to make haste, Sam, but I don't think you can keep your mount if we run." Gus said. "Keep your horse at a trot or below, and I'll stay behind you where I can keep an eye on you." An hour passed. Sam's vision began to blur and his muscles twitch. The pain in his arm, intense, but local at first was spreading and becoming unbearable. Gus caught Sam's reins. "I'm goin' to put you on my mule in front of me, and we'll let ole jawbone go. We need to make some time."

Gus pushed Sam on to the mule and mounted behind him. He spurred the mule into a run. "I think we should be there in an hour, just before sunset."

Darkness was overtaking the little town of Fairy as Gus and Sam came into view of Mutt's and Billy's small frame house. Sam was unconscious and lay across the saddle in front of Gus. Billy met Gus at the gate amidst a whirling troupe of snapping, barking mongrels.

"He's snakebit, Billy. Is Doctor Futselmacher in town?"

"Mutt!!" hollered Billy. "Mutt, go get Doc Fuhlendorf, or this boy might not make it."

Gus and Billy carried Sam into the house and laid him on a small bed on the sleeping porch at its rear.

"That is a bad lookin' bite, Gus", Billy said as he held a lantern over Sam. "There's not much we can do until Doc comes."

Fortunately, Mutt had caught the doctor just before he left to check on one of his patients back in the hills surrounding Fairy. Within a few minutes, Mutt slammed the back door open with the doctor in tow. Doc Fuhlendorf looked at the wound.

"We need to tie this off and bleed it. If there is too much tissue damage from the swelling, we might have to take the hand or even the arm off. We will not know for a few hours." Doc cut an incision around the wound. Thin, bloody fluid drained rapidly into a basin Mutt had placed below his hand. "When he wakes, I'll give him something for the pain, 'cause that is going to hurt like the dickens for some time to come. For now, however, we can just wait and watch."

The men left the room to smoke on the porch. Mutt, whose given name was Murtice, was Billy's wife. She bathed Sam's face with a cool wet rag, and spoke soft, nonsense words to comfort him. Sam's breath was rapid, but he was otherwise motionless. The men stood on the porch, their faces intermittently illumined by the glowing coals of their cigarettes.

Billy looked at Gus who stood a little distance away, then turned to Fuhlendorf.

"What do you think, Doc? Is the boy goin' a make it?" Fuhlendorf was slow to answer, and took a long draw on his Bull Durham and coughed until he was red in the face and his eyes watered. After he gained control of his coughing fit, he replied hoarsely,

"Well, I don't know." He called down the porch to Gus. "Gus, how long was he bit before I got here?"

23

"About two hours, maybe a little less." he guessed. Gus held his hat in his hands and nervously turned the brim like a wheel. "I didn't want to run his horse. I thought it would stir up the poison, and he might not keep his saddle. I finally put him up in front of me. It might've been good to have done it sooner." Billy put his hand on Gus's shoulder.

"You never know what's the right thing until it's all done," he said.

Billy and Gus had been friends since the times they had served together in the ranging company. For several years, they had served under Charlie Travis, the son of William Travis, the ill-fated commander of the Alamo. They had joined just at the close of the Civil War, when the really big fights with the Comanche were past. Both had spent their time chasing small bands of raiders who were better mounted and more informed on the geography of the region. Therefore, neither had managed to do more than fire a shotgun shell or two at the fleeing backsides of the enemy. The closest Gus had come was the close view of the spotted rump of an Indian pony, its tail tied up and decorated with eagle feathers. It had disappeared into the darkness before he could draw his gun from its scabbard. Regardless, Billy's and Gus's many days and nights spent in futile chase had formed a strong bond between them. If Gus was to lose poor Sam, it was good to have Billy with him. He was not sure that the loss would be of much consequence to Mabel or her nieces, or for that matter, to Sam's father, Abbott, who had not been heard from since his departure for the oil fields.

Near daybreak, Doc Fuhlendorf examined Sam. "It looks like we will have to sever the first two fingers, or gangrene will be a certainty. We might be able to save his hand, though." Doc fondly brushed the hair out of the boy's eyes. "I could give him ether, but in his condition, I don't know if he could stand it. I think I shall take advantage of his unconsciousness and do it before he wakes."

Gus and Billy held Sam's arms and feet down, and Doc performed the amputation. His hand was bandaged and tied to the bedpost, to prevent further damage when Sam awoke and the pain set in.

Sam woke near the height of day, sweating and nauseated. Mutt brought the basin and held it by the side of the bed while Sam vomited. Doc Fuhlendorf came in.

"I see our patient is awake." He examined the wound and changed bandages. He poured brown liquid into a tin measuring cup he had retrieved from his bag. "Mutt, this is laudanum. It will be good for the pain, and it will keep him quiet." Sam was able to swallow the dose, and within minutes began to doze.

Around midnight, Sam woke, his hand was throbbing, but the pain had once again moved to a single part of his body. The moon was up. The hills and prairie were lit like daylight. The moonlight was so intense that it seemed to buzz. A mockingbird sang from an elm tree in the back yard. There was no other sound. Sam lay in his bed and listened. He had never seen or heard anything so pure. Mutt heard Sam stir and came to his room. She administered another dose of laudanum.

"Sam, I feel bad that you were comin' with the hope of eating some of my pie, and here you are snakebit, instead.

When you are feelin' up to it, I will make two pies, just for you, and you can sit here in bed like a king and eat 'em, and nobody will say nothin' about it. I'm glad you are here, since Bill and I never had any children of our own. I like takin' care of a child, even if he is pretty well growed up like you."

Yielding to the opium haze, Sam began to doze, but was again taken by the intensity of the moonlight and the singing of the mockingbird. Sam's world had shifted, somehow. His injury was an empty time where he began to imagine that he was changed. It was a place for him to start a new story which could become his life. Being cared for by a woman, who told him that she was glad he was there and had offered him two pies to be eaten in bed, made him feel somehow further from harm than he had before the snake had bitten him. He slept.

Gus's business with Billy was conducted, though it had not been the business considered two years ago. Mabel's finances had deteriorated to the extent that the house and most of its furnishings were to be sold to settle her debts and provide her with income sufficient to see her through her waning years. Mabel would move to Stephenville to reside with her sister, Maybelle. Gus had negotiated room and board from Billy and Mutt until they could find other arrangements. The house was small. Three rooms, a lean-to kitchen and the sleeping porch now occupied by Sam were situated in the folds of the hills on the south side of Fairy. A largish smoke shed was situated at the back of the lot. Gus weighed its potential as living quarters. There was enough room for the two of them, provided they accumulated no more possessions than they had arrived with. The shed had two features which pleased Gus. The floor of the shed was paved in flagstone, which would be easy to sweep and keep the dust down, and the atmosphere was permeated with live oak smoke and the smell of curing hams. He expected that would be enough to put Sam back on his feed.

Sam's convalescence continued through the late summer. He returned to his feed more rapidly than expected, and — true to her word— Mutt produced two pecan pies, one of which Sam consumed in bed. Sam and Gus moved into the former smoke shed. Gus insisted the smell of phantom pork was the thing that brought Sam's appetite back. Though the shed was small and poorly ventilated, the stone floor held the coolness of the night well into the day. On some hot days Sam would lie face down on the floor for the coolness in it. His hand was still a source of discomfort, though it appeared to be healing faster than Doc Fuhlendorf had expected. Sam would remove the bandage and stare at the half moon hole which had replaced his little and ring finger and a portion of the blade of his hand. He would make pinching gestures with his remaining fingers and imagine the limitations he might experience and, more importantly, how his diminished hand would be received when he returned to school.

CHAPTER 4

Summer was drawing to a close and school would begin soon. Mutt began to concern herself with Sam's education. He was entering the 7th grade. Fairy had a school of some reputation, having nine grades and overseen by the namesake of the town, Mrs. Fairy Fort Phelps. Mrs. Phelps was an unusually small woman, the daughter of the founder of the town, Captain Battle Fort. In the early days, school was conducted in the family's home. By the fall of 1912, the school had grown to twenty-two students, two teachers and two rooms. Mutt provided Sam with several shirts and pairs of pants, formerly worn by Billy in his younger and trimmer years and, washed and patched, were hemmed to fit Sam's short legs and arms.

The drought had continued into September. This first day of school, a southwest wind had dragged heat and dust up from the deserts of Mexico, and the light had a dim and brassy quality to it. As Sam drew close to the school, he could smell acrid cigar smoke emanating from the vicinity of the horse stalls near the back door of the school. It occurred to Sam that it must be an impressive cigar to out-smell horse stalls. Several of the older boys leaned against the back wall. An admiring crowd of younger boys watched from a respectful distance. The big boys smoked a fat brown cigar and took turns posing with it. One of the boys, apparently the group's leader, noticed Sam.

"Whatchew lookin' at?"

"Nothin'." replied Sam. "This is my first day at the school."

The boys sauntered over to Sam and encircled him. "Yew wanna drag?" the leader offered Sam the cigar. Sam reached for the cigar with his incomplete hand. The little crowd drew back with a startled gasp.

"What happened to your hand?" asked one of the younger boys. Sam related the story of the ride across the Rocking B, the lizard and the snakebite.

Sam was an instant celebrity. For all of that first day, the boys made Sam surprise the girls by hiding his hand in his pocket, then suddenly brandishing it before them, making them scream. He chased girls and the little boys around the school yard pinching his index and middle fingers like a crawfish, earning him the nickname "Crawdaddy". Sam liked the attention. He was relieved that his wound brought a sort of notorious respect, instead of derision. Sam's notoriety gained him membership in the gang of the three cigar smoking 'big old boys,' led by Oscar Biggerstaff. However, Oscar soon departed after an incident with his teacher, Mrs. Ogden. Oscar had stood at an empty chalk board, pondering on how to begin an arithmetic problem. Mrs. Ogden, a plump and usually genial woman in her early forties, sat watching at her desk. Oscar, trying to impress his audience, ran his fingernails across the chalk board.

"Oscar, quit it!" she demanded. "That makes my skin crawl." said Mrs. Ogden.

"Well, then. How did your butt smell when it passed your face?" replied Oscar, who delivered the line to his admiring audience.

If Oscar had not been occupied with grinning at the snickering faces of his fellow students, he could have saved himself from being grabbed by the ear and hauled to Mrs. Phelps office. Oscar was not seen at school for the remainder of the semester.

In early October, it appeared that the drought might break. The morning sky north and west of Fairy had the blue-black color of a bad bruise. The wind from the south had picked up as if the northern sky was inhaling a big breath before blowing all of the hats in Fairy into the nearest creek. By the time Sam had walked to school, the rumble of not-too-distant thunder made it clear they were in for a big storm.

Miles northwest out on the range north of the Rocking B Ranch, the prairie grasses sighed with the passage of the wind. There, the sky had taken on an ugly greenish tinge and the wind had begun to still. In an instant, a bolt of green lightning snaked out of the overcast and struck the earth, flinging clods and leaving the smell of ozone and smoke. The grasses were lit. Little fingers of flame reached into the bunch grasses and once it appeared that the flame had run out of fuel. Then the wind blew. Embers from many little fires ignited bigger fires which became driven by the increasing speed of the wind. The head of the fire began to pick up speed so that it could outpace a running man, and eventually, a running horse. Whirlwinds of fire and smoke and embers carried the fire beyond its wind-driven front. Jackrabbits, cotton rats, and reptiles of all descriptions fled only to be consumed by the wall of flame, or were lucky enough to find refuge under a ledge or in a hole in the ground.

At ten-o'clock, Mrs. Ogden released the class for recess. Sam looked around for some of the big ole boys who ordinarily lounged by the horse stalls. They were with a small cluster of children at the back corner of the schoolyard looking to the northwest. Sam could see the column of white smoke starkly contrasted against the black sky.

"It's a prairie fire!" exclaimed one of the little boys. The little girls screamed with hand-flailing excitement and ran for the building, while the older boys lingered, feigning disinterest. Mrs. Ogden, led by the hand by a cluster of younger girls, joined the group. The oldest boy was sent to find the town Marshal, who was already riding up the street at a gallop.

"Get those children inside, but leave the big boys with me", he said in a tight but soft voice. Sam, being small, was secretly pleased that he was included with the bigger ones.

Marshal Jack Pickerel, a man just shy of six feet and three hundred pounds, ran to the tool shed of a neighboring house and returned, bearing rakes, shovels, hoes and empty feed sacks.

Gasping between words from the exertion, he said, "You boys bare the soil on the north side of the school, and make it about ten feet wide and do it fast!" Being mostly farm boys, all had spent much time with these tools, and made quick work of the firebreak. Jack returned from the well where he had soaked the gunny sacks.

"I'm gonna light a fire guard on the other side of your line, and you boys hold the fire from the school with these sacks." he said. He picked up a dirt rake and scratched enough dry grass onto it to make a torch. With this he lit the fire guard along the boys' scratch line. The flames began to slowly burn into the wind, and the boys slapped out any creeping fire on the other side. Before long, they had gained more than one-hundred feet of blackened soil.

A bolt of lightning split the sky, and the cedar-clad hill behind the school began to smoke and shoot up fingers of flame. The squat shrubs had spent the dry summer accumulating volatile oils in their needles, waiting for the provocation of an ember to burn to the ground in a matter of seconds. At first, three or four cedars the size of small sheds exploded. Sam gawked from the corner of the school. The fire guard had been constructed to intercept the flame front approaching from the northwest. Now the fire had erupted east. Sam drew a breath to call to the Marshal. At that moment, all the air seemed to be sucked from the school yard and from Sam's lungs. An explosion of flame shattered school windows and sent those children who had not been knocked down running. Jack yelled at the children to get in the middle of the fire guard. The one hundred feet of black might protect them. Men, women and children from the neighborhood emerged from shops and houses and ran for the blackened soil. The advancing headfire from the first lightning strike created a vacuum which pulled the flames from the hill toward them.

All of the children lay face down on the blackened ground and some covered their noses and mouths with bandanas. The smoke was so thick, breathing was difficult and Sam could not see the child beside him. The heat was so intense he thought his clothes would catch fire. The fire front from the northwest reached the fire guard where it overlapped by twenty feet. Sam could hear the screams of those unfortunate enough to seek safety too close to the edge. The fire however, dropped to a smolder at the black, but flames twenty feet high blazed by the unburned corner.

The Marshal led the crowd further into the street, in anticipation of the school catching fire. Fortunately, the fire guard had lessened the intensity of the advancing flame front. Now the fire on the hillside was under the control of the wind and only a small fire backed down the hill toward the buildings of Fairy. Men from town extinguished the little fire with the wet sacks.

Only four people sustained serious injury. Their attention had been focused on the flaming hillside, and, in their attempt to move away from it, had moved too close to the advancing fire front. A mother and her two young children sat at the edge of the fire guard, crying in pain. One of the townsmen lay face down and unconscious. Dr. Fuhlendorf arrived within minutes and the four were loaded onto a passing wagon and delivered to his office. Of those unfortunates, only the man, unknown and a recent arrival, perished. He had inhaled the scorching gases and had suffocated.

The school was blackened, its windows shattered, but it was still standing. Mrs. Ogden gathered her charges and ushered them back to the classroom. Inside, she gathered the paper which had blown from the desks and issued brooms and dustpans to several of the students. Parents, desperate to ascertain the fates of their children, began to arrive before the cleanup was well underway. Mrs. Ogden dismissed those students to their parent's care. Gradually, the crowd of children dwindled to a handful. Sam was among the few. The remaining children lived out in the county, away from town. For a while it appeared that parents had been delayed by distance. However, as the sun began to approach the horizon, Mrs. Ogden looked at this little group with tight lips and moistening eyes. Her change in demeanor seemed to sever the last threads of hope for several of the children. One of the first grade girls began to whimper, and this spread rapidly through the group. Sam, being older and independent, was dismissed to determine the fate of his guardians, but with strict instructions to return to the school should the news be bad.

Sam stepped through the door of the school. The rain, which had looked so promising that morning, had moved south and east. He could smell the distant faint smell of moistened dust on the wind, but in Fairy, only the smell of burned grass and charred wood.

Billy's and Mutt's house was on the south edge of town, a little removed from the other houses, which had picket-fenced yards and flower gardens. It sat at the base of and to the east of a stony hill. Sam could see that the house and smoke shed still stood, but the other outbuildings and corrals had burned. At the distance, he could distinguish two figures standing in the dooryard, but he dared not hope.

CHAPTER 5

A month had passed since the range fire and the loss of Billy. Mutt frequently cried into dishtowels, but Gus had just become more silent. Billy had been buried in the little cemetery north of town; had joined many other old-timers who had seen the country go from buffalo to automobiles. When the fire came, there had not been time to build a fire guard. Gus and Mutt had escaped to an expanse of bare limestone south of the house, but Billy had lingered to gather up the little bit of livestock pastured on the north side of the lot. Mutt and Gus screamed and whooped for Bill to give it up. The stock needed little encouragement to flee the fire, but Billy had a particular concern that a lame old horse was still trapped at the back of the lot. For a short time, it appeared that he had beat the headfire, but in the end, he was outflanked by one finger which turned and joined the head, over-running him. He had just simply disappeared in the flame.

Sam harbored a secret gratitude that it had been Billy and not Gus. Gus was the only tie he had to family and — official or not— without him, he had no guardian. Without Gus, the law might consider him un-tethered. He feared being sent to the orphanage. Orphanage was the specter that had pursued him since the death of his mother and the disappearance of his father. Living in an orphanage was the end of hope; the end of the world. However, what particularly distressed him was that Gus seemed inclined to spend time alone. That did not prevent Sam from following him and watching at a distance.

Gus had developed the habit of sitting on the front steps, chewing tobacco and whittling sticks into toothpicks. Fairy had no saloons, and the front step seemed the best he could do for quiet contemplation. Sam watched Gus from the corner of the house, studying his mannerisms: his ability to spit tobacco juice in a thin stream and past his ponderous moustache; the way he sharpened his knife on the little whetstone he carried. One day he saw Sam watching. He smiled. Sam sat with him.

Gus ruffled his hair and said, "You're a good boy."

At that moment, Sam felt it might be alright, after all, and he would not have to worry about the orphanage.

With Mrs. Ogden's limits of patience better defined, and without Oscar's tutelage in the arts of mischief, Sam applied himself to his studies. He discovered that he could easily grasp a pencil, though he found his penmanship, a former source of pride, had deteriorated. Mrs. Ogden, though often intolerant of adolescent boys, was sympathetic to Sam, who was making steady progress in her class despite what she considered his limitations.

Sam's celebrity waned slightly as the school year progressed. He continued to be admired, but the daily chases by the Crawdaddy became reserved for special occasions and by request only. The Christmas holiday brought the coldest weather seen since the turn of the century. Every morning, Sam went to the cistern and pumped water into a bucket for Mutt to make coffee and biscuits and to wash the breakfast dishes. A long drooly icicle hung from the dripping spigot and Sam had to chip ice before he could pump the water. That morning snow began to fall. Central Texas children did not often have the opportunity to enjoy snow, and the frosty morning brought Fairy's children into the streets and pastures; their tongues extended to catch the snowflakes, and bare hands scraping up dirt and snow to make snowballs. Gus and Mutt came out into the yard to marvel at it. Gus had found a fine woodstove with an Isinglass window on it. He had just managed to install it in the extra room in the house he and Sam now occupied. That night, he fell asleep warm, watching the flames leap behind the little window on the door of the stove.

The next morning, Hamilton County had turned from its customary browns and yellows to dazzling white. The sun shone on the snow with such brilliance that Sam squinted against the shine like it was the brightest August day. Children throughout town had doubled the population of Fairy by making crude snowmen —they lacked practice to produce anything remotely convincing. Sam walked to the center of the town. It was Christmas Eve. The road north of town witnessed a great commotion and, emerging from the valley, spinning tires, kicking up fallen snow, and bearing south toward Sam was a rather worn REO automobile with none other than Oscar Biggerstaff at its wheel. Oscar slid to a stop in front of Sam. Removing the execrable cigar from between his teeth, he smiled down on Sam.

"Wanna go ride?"

Sam looked at the car. "Whose automobile is this, Oscar?"

"Well, let's us just say that my uncle is hung over this morning and don't notice much."

"Awright." replied Sam.

Sam and Oscar sat on that spot for a few minutes, while Oscar worked the gearshift lever, grinding until he could find a position which would move the car. Finally, with a jolting start, Oscar moved the car forward. He and Sam fairly flew out of town and into the bald prairies beyond the hills of Fairy. Because little traffic had moved in that direction, the road, indistinct at the best of times, was invisible under the snow. As a result, Sam and Oscar drove cross country, following fence lines where they were evident, and pushing blindly along through snow, gullies and cedar brakes where they were not. Oscar had a vague idea as to the location of a couple of girls who lived on a little creek which ran to the Leon River. After several hours, they crashed into the door yard of the farm. Oscar knocked on the back door, while Sam waited in the car. Eventually, the back door opened a crack, and Sam saw the curtains in the front window part a fraction of an inch.

Oscar motioned for Sam to follow him through the back door. One of the girls, Darlene, was a pretty brunette of fifteen years, and who seemed to be familiar with Oscar. The other —younger and not as pretty— hid in the dining room and peered at Sam through the crack between an open door and the door jamb. She wiggled her fingers at Sam through the crack in the door.

"Momma and Daddy has gone to the church" said Darlene. Oscar suggested that they take a ride in his automobile.

The girls, at first reluctant, climbed into the back seat of the REO. Oscar placed Sam in the driver's seat where he was instructed to pull one or two knobs while dancing between clutch and some other pedal as Oscar ran to the front of the car to crank. After two or three good cranks, the motor sputtered to life and the car lurched forward. Oscar moved in time to avoid being crushed, but the car ran over his toe, instead.

"You stupid sonofabitch!" yelled Oscar. The car traveled the thirty-five feet necessary to knock down the wall of the sheep shed. The sheep, now visible through the hole in the wall, at first stared blankly across the hood at Sam. It was a rare thing for their surroundings to change so quickly, and it took the sheep a certain amount of time to give it due consideration. Finally, a ram forced his way forward to investigate; paused; made a tolerable pile of steaming sheep pellets and led the flock through the hole to freedom. The girls swooned and cried that their parents would kill them. Not only had they attempted to "run off" with a couple of good-for-nothin' boys, but one of the good-for-nothins' had knocked a hole in Paw's sheep shed!

Sam didn't have a grasp on the proper etiquette for such events so he merely sat speechlessly staring at the steering wheel. Oscar, however, insisted that it was minor inconvenience, and that they should proceed with their plans. Oscar pushed Sam from the driver's seat and took his place. He crammed the gear shift lever into reverse and backed into the yard. After several seconds of grinding, the car moved at an increasingly rapid rate up the road, past the gate and on to the snow-covered county road. Oscar, now chewing on his extinct cigar, declared that he knew an old man down on the river who made and sold liquor. This seemed to resurrect the girls, who had become sullenly quiet in the back seat. Sam had some trepidation about the outcome, particularly concerning how liquor might affect their capacity to get back home. However, he smiled wanly and nodded to Oscar. He liked being one of the big ole boys, but had discovered it carried more risk than just smoking stinking cigars by the horse stables.

Again, Oscar seemed to have only a vague idea where the man lived, but knew for certain that the river was downhill. After an hour of cross-country travel, the car pulled up on the vestiges of a field lane. Sam saw a thin column of smoke rising from the thick woods along the river. Oscar nosed the car toward the smoke, and, dodging trees and for a moment, high centering on rocks buried by snow; they arrived at the shack of Charlie Buck.

Charlie was sitting by his cookstove, so close that his wool pants had begun to scorch and stink. He could not feel the heat because of the two pairs of pants he wore, as well as the union suit he wore beneath, which he changed at least once a year. He thought that he smelled burning hair, and turned to the window more than once to see if someone might be singeing a pig in the neighborhood. He had spent a good portion of the morning shaving his corns with a pocket knife when he heard the roar and rattle of the approaching automobile. He picked up his 30.30, which always leaned within easy reach, pulled on unlaced boots, and met the REO as it slid up to the house. Sam and the girls immediately and quietly suggested that they ask for directions and move on, but Oscar would have none of that.

"Charlie Buck!" Oscar waved familiarly. Charlie glared at him through eyebrows which would have made a tolerable head of hair on a small man. "My uncle is Cole Biggerstaff, and he sent me here to get his whiskey!"

Charlie squinted meanly at Oscar. "He still owes me for the last four bottles he ran off with last month." he grumbled. "Who all is that with 'yuh?" He walked up to the windows of the car and peered in. His breath steamed the glass which he wiped with a greasy shirt sleeve. The girls stared straight ahead, but Sam smiled; said howdy. "I don't know any of these. Where'd y'all come from?"

"We come from Fairy," grinned Oscar, "but we had to pick these ladies up from a creek bottom farm, a mile or two away."

"Let's see yer money." sighed Charlie, who had grown tired from his own suspicion.

Oscar dug his toe into the snow, and said, "Well, my uncle Cole said he would pay for it, but that you were gonna take it in firewood."

"Firewood, Hell!" bellered Charlie, who turned to walk back into the shack.

"Wait a minute!" called Oscar. He ran back to the car and shook down the occupants for any money they had. "We got two bits! What'll that get us?"

"Shot, if you don't get off my land in two minutes." glowered Charlie, who chambered a shell into the 30.30.

"Aw, hell," said Oscar.

The ride home was quieter and somehow shorter than the trip out. Oscar slowed to make the turn into the gate at the girls' house. Before he made the gate both girls jumped from the moving car and ran like deer. The ride to Fairy was even quieter. It seemed to Oscar that none of his objectives for the trip were fulfilled. To Sam, it seemed that nearly all of the disasters had been averted. All, except of course, the hole in Paw's sheep shed and the escape of the flock.

Oscar let Sam off near home. The sun, which had been blinding all day, was a red smudge on the western horizon. Sam feared that he would find the girls' father sitting in Mutt's house waiting to take his expense and inconvenience out on Sam's hide. Instead, Sam found a cedar tree erected in the front room; the smell of ham frying and three old boot socks nailed to the mantle of the fireplace. Each one resembled a distended, sagging scrotum of an old bull. Sam suspected that an apple or orange in each was responsible for the effect, which dragged the toe almost below the firebox.

"Sam!!" cried Mutt, as she wiped her hands on her apron. "I was about to send the hounds out to look for you." She grinned. "Your uncle has found candles for the Christmas tree."

Sam had never seen a Christmas tree, but he had heard the Germans in the area were fond of the practice. He wondered if Mutt was a German. After a Christmas dinner of ham, corn bread, hominy grits and sweet potatoes, Gus struck a match and lit twenty little candles attached to the tree. It was one of the most elegant and beautiful things Sam had ever seen in a house. The candle light made the rude little room seem like a palace, or at least a rich man's parlor.

Mutt sang *Silent Night.* Sam and Gus were silent. Though Mutt wasn't a good singer —she warbled like many old ladies— her voice reminded Sam of the night the moonlight and the singing mockingbird were magic, and his life was changed. There seemed to be no sound but Mutt's voice, and the purity of the candle light was like that of the moon. After a few minutes of silent admiration, Gus pinched each candle out, and then lit the fireplace and the oil lamp. He smiled and pointed to one of the socks on the mantle.

"That one's yours, Sam."

Sam tried to reach in through the top of the sock, but it was mounted high enough to thwart him. He pulled the sock off of the nail, and plunged his hand in. First, he found, wrapped in butcher paper, four pieces of ribbon candy. One was red striped, one yellow, and the others green. Below that, he found a small rectangular box, wrapped in newspaper. Sam sat down by the fire and began to unwrap it. Inside was a shiny new penknife with a bone handle. Sam had never had such a fine gift. Its blade shone like a mirror. Sam repeatedly opened and closed it.

"Well? What do you think?" asked Gus.

Sam smiled with all of his teeth. "Now I can sit with you on the step and chew tobacco and whittle sticks!" Gus laughed, and Mutt commented that he would do well to avoid tobacco chewing.

"It'll make your teeth brown, and the girls won't want to kiss you."

That night, Charlie Buck sat by his cook stove. The stove was full of cedar stumps. Their oil content was high enough to make them mildly explosive. Every two or three minutes, an ashy 'fump' erupted from the stove, rattling stove lids and puffing sparks around the flue. Outside, the wind had picked up. It moaned through the eaves of his small shack and rattled the loose panes of glass in his only window. Had someone looked in on Charlie, he would not have surmised that he was at peace, let alone happy. He rarely drank his own or others' liquor, but Christmas had put him in a celebratory mood. More important, events that day had truly excited him. After the Fairy urchins had departed, slinging mud and snow on his driveway, Charlie had walked down to the edge of the woods to check on his still. A barrel of mash had been turned over. Charlie cursed the neighbor's pigs, which ran wild along the river bottoms. However, a footprint in the snow silenced Charlie. It was the print of the right forepaw of a bear: a big boar.

CHAPTER 6

Charlie Buck was born in 1848, not far from Cowhouse Creek in the southern part of the county. The town of Hamilton was distant, and not much more than a camp. He was just beginning to talk when the Comanche troubles of the 1850's brought much bloodshed and sorrow to the little creek valleys dissecting the prairie. In the fall of 1850, Charlie and his family lived in a dugout on a small tributary of the creek. A small band of the 'people' —for that is what they called themselves— had moved down the valley on a cool fall night. Three houses had been visited, and all of their residents killed — all except Charlie. Something about Charlie had made him seem like a potential Comanche. He was adopted. He was taken to the rolling plains country near the Prairie Dog Fork of the Red River, and until the age of ten, had been a Comanche. Had he stayed a bit longer, he would have been stealing Hamilton County horses and taking Hamiltonian scalps. Captain Snow and a company of rangers raided Charlie's camp and killed as indiscriminately as had the Comanches on the Cowhouse. Charlie did not know nor much appreciate that he was being rescued.

Charlie's family was relatively new to the county and unknown to the countians. They remembered the raids on Cowhouse Creek, and figured that Charlie fit in age and gender to the one assumed captured. However, no one knew the name of the family. Therefore, having lived with and become one of the Comanche, and having uncivilized manners, he was called Buck. More sympathetic people believed he deserved a first name and bestowed Charlie on this skinny, dirty, hostile boy.

Charlie was given a cot in the shed of Bertrand Forsythe, the only Quaker living in the county. At first, Charlie sat in the dark shed, waiting to die. Though he resembled his new captors, he was unaware of any racial kinship. He thought they looked like corpses which had lain in the water too long. Eventually, it was evident to him that they did not intend to kill him, but he believed he would be infected with whatever it was that made them look so sick.

Charlie was a silent boy, which put him in good stead when the few Friends gathered for silent contemplation. However, his silence impeded his progress at school, particularly when he was accused of various acts of mischief. The accusations were met with silence and averted eye, which schoolmarms interpreted at best as sullenness and at worst a prelude to aggression. The school's children soon learned that blame was easy to place on Charlie Buck, and as a result, the school principal suggested that a less formal education might suit him better. Mrs. Bertrand Forsythe was given charge of his education. It was her view that Charlie's years of deprivation by the Indians had damaged his mind. Therefore, Charlie's education consisted of a weekly reading and arithmetic lesson. Outside of this, a few chores, bed and meals, Charlie's time was his own.

A little creek at the end of the Forsythe's grain field was his first refuge. Charlie hid inside the little gallery of hackberry, wild plum and cottonwoods that fringed the stream's edge. His band had camped by many such little streams, and in the winter, the ponies ate the cottonwood bark so that the trees died. He had spent many summers wading and swimming in little creeks; catching tadpoles and the little sunfish which lived in the pools. However, the creeks he knew had sandy and clay bottoms. On those, his footsteps made the water brown and red and murky. The mud squished up between his toes. This creek had a solid white stone bottom, and in the riffles moss grew thick and slick. He spent much of his time with wet britches and a sore butt.

Charlie Buck called his forays into the forests hunting trips, for the benefit of the Forsythes who had decided that there was little remediation that could be done. Besides, 'hunting trip' sounded wholesome enough that Mrs. Forsythe cheerfully provided Charlie salt, bacon and flour, and an old blanket to take with him. Mr. Forsythe loaned him an old black powder shotgun and a hand axe. He assumed that any boy reared by the Comanches was sufficiently martial that no further training would be needed. So, in his twelfth year —the dawn of the Civil War— Charlie struck out on his own. Many boys, even tough farm boys, would have started such an adventure with daring. However, time, distance, hardship and separation would have most back home within a few weeks. For Charlie, there was really no place to return to. He had lived among his own race long enough to know that he was not Comanche, and had lived among the Comanche long enough to know he could not live among the whites. He now preferred his own company. Charlie rolled his flour, salt and bacon into his blanket and hung it across his shoulder like a bandolier. He hung his axe on his belt and picked up the shotgun. Bertrand Forsythe stood in the shadow of his front porch and watched him cross the little grain field and disappear into the woody scrim of the creek. He did not expect to see him again, but it was a thought he would never reveal to his wife, who had already begun to have reservations.

The first thing Charlie did when he reached the creek was take off the heavy laced shoes he had been given. He hid them under the stream bank. He had no particular gripe about his shirt and pants, but he had long wished he could lose his underwear, which were long, woolen and itchy. Having shed these irksome burdens, Charlie began his descent down the little creek. It was early spring, and the plums had, within the last day or so, burst into flower. It occurred to him that all the creeks he had known had plum trees, though they looked different in different parts of his world. He had helped his mother gather July plums on the Brazos, when he was young and not expected to play war. He missed her. Bees of all descriptions made the air hum. The little creek had as much water as it could hold, and had recently had more. Twiggy debris hung from the branches of many of the little trees. The creek joined a larger stream, and at this confluence laid a pool. He could see the illumined backs of sunfish in the clear water. He was hungry. The People rarely ate fish in lieu of more respectable fare, but Charlie was partial to it. He slid into the water without making a ripple. He spotted a small school close to the shore. Suddenly, flailing his arms and making a wake with his advancing body, he sloshed three startled fish onto the shore. He gave each a blow with the butt of his axe and prepared to eat them. He was never too delicate to spurn heads, tails and guts. All were good nourishment. He pulled a flint and steel from his pocket, and built a small fire to cook the fish. While he waited for the fire to burn down to coals, he pulled clay from the stream bank and began to coat the fish in thick layers. When the fire was ready, he placed these in the coals and found some shade. The banks of the larger stream were covered by tall pecans and hackberry trees. The catkins of the pecan flowers floated on the water and were investigated by fish and turtles. The day was warm and mellow, and he ate and dozed in the dappled sunshine.

It took Charlie almost a week to get deep into the Leon River bottoms. He followed the water from one small stream to the next larger. Eventually, this led him to the river bottoms. The little plums and hackberry trees were replaced by bur oak, water oak and hickories. The canopy of foliage stood almost one hundred feet above his head. Greenbrier and grasses carpeted the damp soil under the trees. River bottom forest like this was unknown to Charlie, and even the biggest woods along the upper Brazos looked like scrub in comparison. The air in the forest was thick. When he filled his lungs, the air bore the burden of the living things in the forest: mold, dead leaves, the live exhalations of trees and grasses, live fish, dead fish, and water. He built a brush arbor and prepared himself for a long stay. The weather had turned wet, and walking the wet clay along the river became a chore. Mosquitoes were so thick that his exposed arms, a mass of mosquito bodies, looked gray and fuzzy. Charlie, though, was tolerant of physical discomfort, and the itchy bites gave him something to do at night. His days were spent in the river channel. In the shallows, he felt under logs and ledges, looking for catfish and other edibles. Once, a large mudcat took his arm up to the elbow, and would not release him until he got to the bank and banged on the fish's head with the butt of the axe. Charlie smeared himself with fish fat to repel mosquitoes, but the People only used bear grease. Black bear tallow made a fine ointment for shiny hair, an insect repellent, seasoning for food, a preservative and water repellent for all leathers, and in essence was almost as useful as buffalo. Unfortunately, recalled Charlie, this fact

51

sometimes made for uncomfortable relations with their friends, the Kiowa, many of whom considered bears big medicine and would not mention the word bear let alone enjoy smelling its rendered fat emanating from one's body or breath.

Black bears were still common along the Leon, as were panthers. At night Charlie frequently heard the latter scream. When a panther called from the river bottom, the sound reverberated so, that he was sure the cat was as big as a bull. Those nights, he kept a fire going until sunrise. He saw a few buffalo, mostly old bulls. He watched them graze the grassy bottoms just beyond the skirt of woods. The buffalo had become so scarce that none of the bulls had likely seen or smelled a cow in years, but they still —out of habit, he supposed— sparred for dominance. One old bull, the biggest of the group, returned frequently to his favorite wallow. He spent a few hours each day dusting, and at the end of each roll, would urinate in his wallow. Charlie noted younger and smaller bulls sneaking a roll in the wallow to pick up a bit of big bull perfume. Maybe to fool the cows, he thought. A fat buffalo hump would go good and the hides would be useful as well, but bulls could be dangerous, and the meat was too tough to be eaten. The bears, however, intrigued him, and though he ultimately wanted to take one, he was more interested in getting to know one first.

Every day, Charlie walked five or six miles of the river bottom, crossing as frequently as he could, to find bear tracks. He often found tracks a few weeks old and older. However, it was not until fall that he picked up a new trail. Not far from his camp lay a grove of bur oaks, and by November, the ground was littered with acorns. The bear was a young sow, and he could tell that she had come some distance upstream to use the grove. A short distance from his camp, he could see that the bear had stopped and twisted her body in the direction of his camp. He imagined her testing the air. She had caught his scent, which he supposed smelled of dirty boy, seasoned with the tang of rancid fish oil. He smelled like something tasty. She turned back toward the grove, however, and continued until she came to the first bur oak, where she rubbed her rump against the bark, leaving tufts of brown-tipped black hair. However, after eating and relieving herself of several large turds, she left the way she had come.

It was foggy the following morning. Charlie chose a line of scrub close to the oak grove and settled in. He had left the shotgun and all of his clothes at camp, and had smeared himself with white sage to mask his scent. He wanted to watch her. He lay on his belly and wriggled until he was almost covered in oak leaves. For a while, he slept. Scolding chickadees woke him and told him to look in the direction of their ruckus. The bear's woolly back loomed over the scrim of weeds and grasses along the trail. The mist had frosted her brown fur and Charlie could see the beads of water rolling down her sides. She chuffed, stood on her hind legs and sniffed in the direction of his hideout. Despite the sage and the abandonment of clothes, she still sensed him. To his relief, the bear continued to amble toward the grove. For an hour, he watched her scratch her rump, feed lustily on acorns, relieve herself and amble away. This time, however, she turned her head toward Charlie and stared, silent- as still as a stump.

Charlie realized with a start that he had bedded next to a large tangle of dewberry vines. The fruit was mostly gone, but those few lingering berries were black and sweet.

She ambled toward his hiding place and began eating. As she slowly chewed each berry, her eyes glowed with something approaching ecstasy. He was surprised at the delicacy with which she ate. Apparently, a dewberry was a fine food requiring rapt concentration to achieve full appreciation. The bear slowly browsed closer and closer to Charlie. When the bear had come within six feet of his head, she growled, lowered her head, and began to force it through the brambles separating them until her nose was a few inches from Charlie's face. Her breath smelled like a mixture of dewberries, nuts and fish carrion, which was precisely what she had eaten for breakfast. As his life flashed before his eyes, Charlie wondered what he would smell like on her breath after she had eaten him. He wondered what kind of scat he would make. However, the bear windily sniffed his head, chuffed, and continued browsing. When she reached the end of the bramble, she slowly walked its length, checking for any berries she had missed. Since his close call, she had henceforth ignored Charlie, and now waddled away, satisfied.

Charlie lay briefly without moving. He had held his breath for so long that he gasped as though he had been underwater. Though scared, his desire to find her bedding ground was too intense to abandon his plans. The sky was preparing to rain, and he did not want to seek a diminished trail. About mid-day, Charlie left his hide-out and began to search for the bear's trail. The soil was soft, and the trail was easy to find and follow. It ran a straight course parallel to the river channel. She seemed to have a destination in mind. Charlie remembered his uncle, Two Bellies. He was a great tracker. For entertainment, he tracked the great blue herons which waded along the Brazos one day, and flew to the Trinity the next. He knew individual herons and tracked them throughout their lives. He believed that he would one day leave the earth as a heron, and, unlike Charlie's other relatives, approved of his fondness for fish. He thought maybe Charlie, too, would be a heron tracker. Two Bellies taught Charlie to age tracks, to interpret the mood and physical health of the animal, as well as what its intent was. However, Two Bellies seemed to know things about his prey that tracks could not deliver. He could predict their future.

The November afternoon sky was turning from a muddy gray to dark slate. Night was not far. Charlie had moved slowly, reading the sow's tracks as he went. She had not moved rapidly, but with purpose. Maybe she was trying to reach shelter before the rain started. Charlie was naked and cold. The trail dropped from the river terrace to a flat just a few feet above the water. An old oak had been uprooted in a wind storm, leaving a bear- sized hollow in the space the roots had once held. In the dim light, her eyes shown from the back of the little cave. She was watching him. She coughed, and the little lights blinked out.

The wind had stilled, and Charlie smelled the damp calm that precedes snow. He was cold and decided to return to his camp and settle in for the weather. Now he knew her habits. Now he knew where to find her. There was no hurry. The snow fell without wind all night. In the morning, snow had covered the ground and had settled in the branches of the trees so delicately that Charlie thought his own breath would be sufficient to knock it down. The forest was so quiet; the sound of his heart beating in his ears was distracting. He built a small fire and ate some smoked fish and dried plums from his foraging the creek beds the past summer. He picked up the shotgun, and considered taking her before she moved too far from her bed. Charlie had melted down some buckshot and had forged two heavy slugs. He would have two chances. He put on all of the clothes he owned. He regretted not bringing those despised wool drawers with him. Instead, he stuffed his pants and shirt with dried grass. It would not be long before he had a bearskin coat.

For his ambush, he chose a thicket of greenbrier and old rough dogwood. His breath steamed, but he was certain that he had her.

CHAPTER 7

Shortly after the new year began, the girls' paw finally paid a visit on Sam, Gus and Mutt. The paw was George Carpenter, who was taller than Gus, and far bigger around. He wore bib overalls which he left unbuttoned at the waist to accommodate his barrel-like physique. He had a long dirty-yellow beard, and squinty eyes. His manner was brusque. He demanded that Sam recount the misadventure of Christmas Eve before his guardians. As the story unfolded, Sam was certain that he would be flayed and sent to a reformatory if not an orphanage. Though the loosed sheep flock and the hole in the sheep shed was the first malfeasance addressed, the man glared at Sam from behind his fat eyelids and questioned him as to the state of his daughters' purity. The latter was dismissed when it was evident that Sam was too naïve to get the drift of his indirect, but obvious, inquiry. All that remained was to determine Sam's penance. The sheep flock had long ago been retrieved and the hole repaired. Carpenter did not want Sam anywhere near his daughters, or his sheep, so it was determined that Sam would 'shepherd' Carpenter's large turkey herd following dismissal of school in the spring. Turkey ranching appeared to be an up and coming business which Mr. Carpenter had embraced whole-heartedly. He had assembled a herd of five hundred twenty-five turkeys, which he counted daily.

For a while after the meeting, Mutt looked away when Sam entered the room. Gus grinned and shook his head, looking at the floor. "Shee." is all he had to say. However, the household returned to normal in a week.

School passed slowly that spring. Wet weather followed the Christmas snows. The roads both in and —more unfortunately— out of Fairy had become impassable. Gus told Sam that the rain was "puttin' the seasoning in the ground," but it seemed like it had drained all the spice out of Sam's life. The last week of school, however, the sky shone blue, and an end of school party was organized. Mothers — many in attendance— had brought such an array of food that it was inconceivable that it could all be consumed in a day. Candies, fruit, pies, cakes and sandwiches were laid up on old school doors taken off their hinges and perched between saw horses. The big ole boys, including Oscar Biggerstaff, kept their distance and smoked a rancid cigar. Their horses were tied to the burned up old cedars and live oaks and they kept eyeing something large, white and noisy dangling from a tree.

"You didn't bring a horse?" Oscar sneered. "They's gonna be a goose pull — didn't ya know?"

"No." Sam shrugged. He had never heard of one, but did not want to appear unsophisticated among the worldly big boys.

Oscar said, "Well, you can take your turn on mine, but if you win, I go home with half the goose!"

Sam soon discovered that the riders would attempt to ring the neck of a goose, tied by his feet to a tree limb while galloping by at full speed. The idea was to decapitate him. The winner would take a fresh goose home for dinner, not to mention the great admiration of the assembly for his outstanding horsemanship. That Oscar would share his horse and the prize struck Sam as generosity unexpected from a boy with six brothers and sisters and little food on the table. On the other hand, Sam supposed, it would double his chances of getting home with something to eat.

In the time it took to consume the sandwiches and confections, the goose had worked itself into a state of flaccid exhaustion. This bode well for the contestants, who might not have to grab a moving target. However, the goose warily continued to follow the movement of boys and horses. It panted through a parted beak and with an eye fixed on Billy 'Teeth' McGum —so named for his lack of dental hygiene— who was to be the first rider. Teeth looked at the goose through his eyebrows, fixed his target; tossed away a well chewed toothpick, and spurred his horse into a gallop. The goose's eyes widened, and at the moment Teeth reached for his neck, the goose flapped wings spanning almost six feet, knocking Teeth to the ground. Oscar laughed so hard, he had a coughing fit which put *him* on the ground. Several mothers added to Teeth's mortification by picking him up and dusting him off. Oscar pushed Sam toward his horse, a dirty white gelding who was the tallest horse Sam had ever seen. Oscar pushed Sam up into the saddle and adjusted the stirrups. Sam's legs stuck out at such an absurd angle that even some of the mothers snickered behind their hands. When the signal was given, Sam flapped his legs and shook the reins, but the horse did not move. Oscar cursed and slapped the horse on his rump. The horse took off at a gallop but at a right angle to the target. Sam lay down on the horse's neck and could not see for the mane whipping his face. The wind and lashing mane made his eyes water. He kept them tightly shut. The horse jumped little creeks and ran in and out of gullies for almost twenty minutes before he found an overhanging limb low enough to rid himself of Sam, who hit a spot on the ground hard enough to knock the breath out of him, but not hard enough to kill him. The horse continued to run. Sam could see his white rump getting smaller and smaller as he disappeared into a cedar brake. Oscar, red faced, arrived on Teeth's little pony, and cursed Sam for being such a panty waist and losing his horse.

"You know what yer goin' to do now?" he snarled. "You are going to go chase that horse for the rest of the day until you bring it back!" Sam reached for the reins of Teeth's horse, but Oscar backed the horse away. "And you're goin' to do it afoot!"

Sam climbed the hill into the cedar brake where Oscar's horse, Gallopin' Godfrey, had disappeared. The horse's excitement, combined with the invigorating run, had loosened Godfrey's bowels to the extent that he left an easy trail. Sam found him quietly grazing a grassy opening in the cedars. He caught his reins, and with some trouble mounted him. The horse walked placidly back to the school. Sam's appearance on the edge of the schoolyard elicited much relief from the cluster of mothers, and a smirk from Oscar, who stood holding the lifeless goose by the feet. He had won the contest on Teeth's horse. Teeth argued that he was owed half the goose, but the argument seemed to be lost on Oscar, who brandished the dead goose at Sam.

The first day of June, Sam caught Billy's old mule, packed a bedroll and a few supplies and retraced his trip to the Carpenter's dooryard. The sun shone bright and the leafy hollows, the creeks and green meadows beckoned him. However, he kept the mule at a steady walk. The Carpenter's house and environs looked far worse than they had covered with snow. A low fence enclosed the front yard, which was full of chickens and chicken poot, and void of grass. A trash pile lay by the back door, and the air smelled of cesspool. George Carpenter shambled down the back steps and watched Sam approach.

"Well, I didn't know if you'd come." He sneered while he chewed up the remains of a biscuit.

After he swabbed the remnants from his back gums with an index finger, he crooked a doughy finger at Sam. He dismounted and followed the man at a respectful distance. The turkey shed was a low dark contraption at the back of the lot. Sam had found the source of the cesspool smell. The turkeys were a mixed lot. Some were dark, almost black, while others were snow white. The smell and the noise were equally deafening.

"You're going to use your own mule." he said picking at bits of unchewed biscuit in his beard. "I ain't got the inclination to lend you one."

He proceeded to tell Sam that his job would be to herd the turkeys out to pasture. The job would entail following them to prevent their exiting the farm, and to prevent varmints from molesting them. Just before sunset, he was to turn the herd around and march them back to the enclosure. He could sleep in the turkey shed or on the grounds as he chose. Mrs. Carpenter would set his breakfast and dinner on the stoop for him. He was, under no circumstances, to dine with, talk to, look at or otherwise flirt with his daughters. The same rules applied to his sheep.

After another hour of instruction, Sam picked up a long cane pole, which would serve as his shepherd's crook, and mounted his mule. Carpenter opened the gate and the turkeys filed out.

"I know ever bird here by name," he said. "I want ever one of 'em back before sunset." One old tom turkey seemed to know the routine fairly well, and led the herd in a direct path east of the homestead and into a pasture. Sam assumed a position in the drags, and tried to imagine he was driving a real herd to Abilene or Dodge. The fantasy briefly damped the humiliation, but it was hard to maintain. He was glad that none of his friends —particularly the big ole boys— were likely to come out this far, especially in light of the Christmas mishaps.

The turkeys foraged as they hiked, stirring up grasshoppers and a million other bugs which hopped, leapt, and flew to get out of the way of the ravening beaks. The birds followed the edge of a ravine cloaked in scrub oak. Sam heard a rattlesnake buzz, but the turkeys passed by with little concern. Suddenly, the herd turned into the brush and began to follow a narrow turkey-sized path through the thicket. Sam was not willing to push the mule through it, and, as rapidly as the mule would move, he circled the head of the ravine and met the turkeys on the other side. After an hour of hiking, Sam found the property line. Three strands of droopy barbed wire occasionally tacked to widely spread cedar posts and trees identified the eastern line of the Carpenter holding. Sam poked at the old tom, who began to veer slightly to the north. Thus began the march to the north property line. Hours later, the herd crested a limestone knoll which commanded a view of the range of the Rocking B, which over several miles, sloped gently to the woods along the Leon River. Sam had not seen the ranch since the day the snake bit him. Despite its unpleasant association, Sam thrilled at its aspect. The prairie fire the past fall had burned up the dead matted grass, releasing abundant new growth. The grass, dense as dog hair and a foot high, was a green Sam had not seen before. The breeze worked its way across thousands of acres, turning the silvery undersides of the leaves up to the sky. Sam watched grass move so long, the ground appeared to crawl around him. As he turned to the west to follow the herd, its attendant insect cloud was overrun with barn swallows. One hundred feet above the swallow cloud, night hawks dove into the spiraling mass, and above that, a red-tailed hawk circled. Sam thought it looked like a living tornado ascending into the clouds. As the sun became low on the horizon, Sam pushed the herd toward home, and after an hour of coaxing, found George Carpenter waiting for him on the edge of the east pasture. Carpenter was true to his word, and spent almost an hour counting birds.

"Look for your supper on the back door stoop in about an hour." he said. "Leave the cup and plate there when you are finished." His silence regarding the herd made Sam assume they had come back intact.

Sam found his tin plate piled high with grits, greens, and turkey. He sat on the step and listened to the rattle of plates and talk inside. He recognized Darlene's voice, but could not hear what she said. George Carpenter was doing most of the talking, and even at the distance, Sam could tell he talked with his mouth full. He ate the food quickly and washed it down with well water. The sun was down, and there would

63

be little light left to find a place to sleep. The turkey shed was too foul to sleep in, and even if it had been clean, the noise would keep him up all night. Sam found a shed with a door. Inside he found feed of various descriptions. He rearranged the sacks to make a bed, and spread his blankets on them. The June night was typical — hot and humid. He lay and watched the stars through the narrow doorway. They wavered and blinked in the humid sky. Sleep overtook him, but not before he was startled by a rat bounding across his face. Sam concluded he had oriented his body so that he lay in a regular run, so, he folded himself crosswise in the narrow space.

The next morning, Sam was awakened by the sound of someone making water against the wall of the shed. He poked his head out just as George Carpenter was buttoning up.

"I want you to get started early," he stretched. "You were late gettin' them in yesterday. Too close to sunset when the coyotes and bobcats wake up."

Sam ate his biscuit astride the mule. He began to move the herd toward the pink horizon. This routine continued for several weeks. The real heat had begun, and the turkeys began kicking up a little dust as they made their rounds.

One morning, Sam sat astride his mule, and ate his bite as he moved his herd east toward the ravines. As he descended, the air cooled a little, and it smelled like limestone and sweet cedar. He wished he could stay with it. However, the herd moved on. By noon, heat waves shimmered along the tops of the ridges. The turkeys moved slowly and lingered in the scant shade provided by the few trees. Sam was concerned that he would be unable to get them back to the shed before dusk. He had cached several old pickle jars beneath the cedars and under the ledges in the ravines. Each contained a gallon of water, covered by a little cheesecloth. For the hot days, he always had reliable water, though it tasted faintly of pickle juice. On this day, his shirt had crusted with sweat, and he had used up his canteen. The water in the pickle jar was cool, and he held the heavy jug against his head for the coolness in it. The water tasted of sweet limestone, and pickles. To Sam, it was a tasty combination. Sam sat in the shade of a limestone ledge, and watched the herd as it found a meadow below to search for grasshoppers. The ledge still held a little dampness from the last rain. Sam reclined for the benefit of the cool and immediately fell asleep.

Sam gasped at the clap of thunder that woke him. The air smelled like wet dust and the turkeys, which seemed absorbed in picking grasshoppers moments before, had disappeared. Though partially obscured by the thunder head, the sun told him that he had slept into the early afternoon. Sam had some trouble finding his mule, which had fled the thunder. Once mounted, he began to track his herd. Raindrops the size of silver dollars began to fall, kicking up little spumes of dust as they hit the ground. Any fresh turkey track would be wiped out before he could find them, he thought. He followed the regular route of the turkeys, but found no sign until he saw several feathers caught in the fence separating the Rocking B from the Carpenter land. The land on the north side of the fence was guarded by Ruder Bilch's cowhands, and it was with trepidation that he tied his mule to the fencepost and began cutting wire.

The grass of the Rocking B range was of sufficient height that the passage of the turkey herd was evident. The trail became dim when it crossed a bare limestone glade on the hilltop, but appeared in the grass of the slopes. Sam followed the trail downhill until he came to the river bottom. As he entered the forest, the rain began to fall in earnest, pummeling the leafy canopy and making a din that startled Sam. The forest floor was an impenetrable tangle of greenbrier. The mule refused to go further. Sam sat down in the duff and thorns and cried. The sun was not far from setting and he began to gather the driest wood he could find. He prepared to camp and continue the search in the morning. If he was lucky, he could get the herd back to the Carpenter farm and be fired rather than killed.

Sam was awakened by a kick that caught him just below the ribs of his back. The sun had barely penetrated the foggy, dripping forest. Sam struggled to his feet, but his legs were kicked from under him. His assailant, one of Bilch's cowboys, stood over him, showing a toothy sneer stained with tobacco. The other man was standing by the mule, rifling through Sam's saddlebags.

"Here they are!" He held up a pair of rusty fence pliers. "So *you* are the fence cutter." He spat tobacco juice on Sam's pants and straddled him, grabbing both of his hands. He started and let go of Sam's incomplete hand.

"Sonofabitch! He's missing most of this one!"

The man dropped the pliers and dragged Sam through the remnants of his campfire. They tied his wrists and threw the rope over a low-hanging limb. The cowboy with the stained teeth looped the other end over the horn of his saddle and pulled Sam off the ground, so that his toes just touched the ground. The other man picked up a wrist-sized piece of firewood.

He said, "I'm gonna show you what we do with fence cuttin' little turds like you."

The first blows almost broke Sam's knees. When the man was satisfied with the damage, he began to work about his ribs and his kidneys. Sam screamed, but each scream was cut short with a blow to the mouth. Blood began to pool beneath him. The man with the stained teeth was jealous of a turn and grabbed the bludgeon.

"I'm gonna beat in his damn head." he snarled. The crack of a rifle dropped the man just as he wound up to deliver the final blow. The second shot knocked the other out of one boot, though he managed to mount his horse and flee.

Charlie Buck cut Sam down. He cut little saplings and stripped the bark from them and twisted together a small travois. He gently lifted Sam, who was mumbling and barely conscious and placed Sam on blankets he had laid in the travois. The mule was uncomfortable with the load and danced some, but soon settled in to a plodding gate which jarred Sam's damaged knees with every step. Charlie shouldered his rifle and led the mule into a part of the forest which had a high canopy and little undergrowth. Every few steps, the mule slipped on the riverbank mud, but soon, a game trail appeared which made for easier travel and paralleled the river for miles. They arrived at Charlie's cabin by mid-afternoon. He left Sam in the travois and rummaged around his camp and cabin until he had what he required for an extended expedition.

By nightfall, Charlie had made camp in a part of the river forest he had not visited for years. He made a small lean-to, and prepared bread by wrapping sticks with dough, and placing them over the fire. Sam was conscious, but wished he wasn't. The pain in his knees had subsided, but his head hurt him so intensely he was sick. The rain returned and the dampness made his body ache. Charlie bound up Sam's head and knees. It was all the medicine he cared to apply. If Sam survived the night, he decided, he would probably recover.

He moved away from the lean-to and under the forest canopy. Most of the rain hit the leaves and ran down the trunk of the tree he sat against, wetting his back. He lit a small pipe, and began to assess the situation for the first time that day. He wished he had dropped the second of Bilch's cowhands, and was sure he had made it to the Sheriff or to Bilch to report ambush and cattle rustlers. There would be little chance for him, and only slightly better for Sam. The rain would help some with the trail, and by the time a Sheriff's posse was assembled it would have been too dark to start. However, Charlie expected to see more Rocking B hands before the day was through. Charlie pulled his Winchester from its scabbard and began wiping it down with a little oil, checking the action of the lever, looking down its sights. When he was finished, he did the same with his old Sharp's .50 caliber. These old rifles and a shotgun were the only weapons he ever carried, in addition to a sharp knife. He thought it was likely all three would be used before the week was out.

CHAPTER 8

Bilch's cowboy had taken a bullet in the chest, and was foaming blood from his mouth by the time he rode into Rocking B headquarters. Bilch was able to determine that he and his partner had been bushwhacked by rustlers before the man rattled his last breath. He sent a contingent of eight cowhands after the fallen comrade and to locate the offenders if possible. Bilch left to retrieve the Sheriff.

After some time, Bilch's hands found the fallen cowboy. The single bullet had struck him just below his right eye. The flies crawled across his face and open eyes; the buzzards waited in the trees above him. He had been a good friend to several of the hands, and they wept at his loss. He was not more than twenty, and far more popular than had been his partner, who was middle-aged and unpleasant. He would not be as missed. They wrapped the boy in a blanket and placed him across the back of an extra horse. Four of the men, primarily the boy's mourners, left with the body to see him properly interred. They discussed his funeral arrangements as they rode, and vowed vengeance on any man who could do such a thing.

At dawn, Charlie tore down the lean-to and scattered it. He put Sam on the travois and began to move south, downriver into denser woods. Bur oak, water oak, and pecan trees formed the high canopy he had known as a boy. He began to recognize this part of the river. Some of the oldest trees —gnarled with peculiar shapes— were familiar to him. He guessed that there could be five or ten thousand acres of bottomland hardwood left in the stand. The timber had been gently used, and the wetness of the ground had prevented its wholesale cutting. He was near the place he had taken his first bear.

The air was wet from the recent rains, and though well shaded, sweat stood on Charlie's brow. His sleeves and Sam's face were gray with mosquitoes. Charlie descended the steep bank of the river and waded into the murky water. He reached under the bank and searched under fallen logs until he emerged with a catfish. He rapidly skinned it and put the flesh into a pouch with fresh leaves. With the fat side of the fish skin down, he wiped his face and exposed skin, then began to work on Sam. The smell woke him and made him gag.

"Simmer down," Charlie snarled. "This will even turn the stomach of them blood-suckers."

Charlie began unloading the mule and assembling the gear next to Sam's travois. Finally, he untied the travois and laid the contraption and Sam flat on the ground. He swatted the mule who ran only a few yards and began to graze.

"We are going to travel by water for a while, boy. There's no use in leavin' a trail for them hot headed sons-a-bitches to follow."

Despite the rain, the Leon was still down to its summer flow. Charlie lashed the travois to some logs and, with Sam and gear on top, guided it down the river. Sam felt slightly better, and lying on his back, watched the overhanging canopy of trees pass by. Kingfishers perched on the most prominent overhanging limbs, and Sam watched as they swooped into the water for a meal. River otters, beavers, and snakes of many descriptions made ripples in the water.

Charlie did not seem bothered by the prospect of encountering a water moccasin. Had it not been for his pain, he would have considered this one of the most enjoyable trips of his life.

After two days in the river, they pulled out where the river bank was not steep. Charlie rifled through the gear and found his guns, a few blankets, and a side of greenish bacon. The rest he dragged into the underbrush and scattered.

"Well boy. I hope you can walk now, because we have a whole lot of walkin' to do."

Sam hobbled until he found a stout limb on the ground. He tested it, and found it helped, though his pain and stiffness was still plenty. Charlie found an old trail that led up the creek branches away from the river. The heat and mosquitoes were almost intolerable to Sam, but, by the second day, they appeared to have at least eluded the posse. Each night, Charlie climbed the tallest tree he could find, and scouted northwest for the faint glow of campfires. After a few more days, he was convinced they had lost their pursuers.

Fairy had divided into two factions: those who believed Sam had fallen in with bad company and had turned outlaw, and those who believed he had been a victim of outlaws. George Carpenter sided with the former. He reported to the Sheriff that Sam had stolen his turkey herd and that Oscar Biggerstaff and his ilk were behind him.

"Not much of a stretch for him to move from turkeys to cows, I suppose." he sneered.

No one was sure exactly who he had fallen in with, since only those who bought illegal liquor were the only ones who knew Charlie Buck, and it did not surprise them when he disappeared, nor were they inclined to announce the association. Mutt and Gus had become silent on the matter and rarely spoke. Gus had spent more than a week on the Leon in search of sign, but he feared he might lead Bilch's men to Sam, if Sam had in fact fallen in with a bad crowd. It did not seem likely, and he told Mutt so.

"Sam is a good boy. I knew that the first day I saw him. He always did the best he could, so I don't suppose he would go bad that quick."

The County Sheriff showed little interest in pursuing rustlers or saving Sam. He organized Bilch's posse, but only rode with them till the heat and damp got more than he could bear.

After a few weeks, the focus of conversation in Fairy had moved from speculation about Sam to the improvement in the weather —rain had finally returned— and the recovery of range grasses. When Sam's disappearance reached the three-week mark, Gus decided he should try to contact Abbott Wood, though he did not know where to write. The last Gus heard of him, he had worked in the oilfields near Purdon, in east Texas. Gus whittled the end of a little stub of pencil and wrote as well as he could. Mutt, who had finished sixth grade, offered to help, but Sam was his charge. Not Billy's. Not Mutt's. He had failed. Gus looked up from the paper on his knee.

"Writing this is a waste of paper, anyway, Mutt, but at least I can say I tried." After two attempts, and two returned letters, he abandoned the effort.

On the Rocking B, Bilch and his hands had not forgotten the loss of the young cowboy and the weathered old hand. Bilch, though, was puzzled that all of the cattle had been accounted for. Before either of his hands were buried, the rest of the crew rode the fifty thousand acres for days doing a head count. Only fifteen were missing, and at least that many would be hiding in the brush, were bogged and dead in the river, or wandered through the fence. In Bilch's calculus, the loss of livestock overshadowed the loss of a couple of replaceable hands, and one was old and the other inexperienced. The miscreants would show up eventually, and when they did, no judge or jury would be necessary.

CHAPTER 9

Sam's injuries slowly healed, but after a month, he was able to walk on his own and help Charlie with camp chores. Charlie had found a tree which —having been uprooted along the bank of a little creek— made a small cave. He dug it larger with his knife and the tin plate he ate from each night. Eventually, the cave was big enough for the two of them to stretch out in. Roots hung from the ceiling and tickled Sam's face at night, and daddy longlegs clung to the walls. Further, Sam did not like the idea of living in a potential snake den. Though he had not seen rattlesnakes in the woods, copperheads and cottonmouths were abundant.

The weather had turned mild, and the leaves were turning yellow and copper. Sam surmised it was toward the end of September. Charlie's mood had improved some, and he began addressing Sam by his name when he spoke to him, which was seldom. The camp diet was improving as deer, fattened on acorns, began to replace catfish as their main sustenance. One early morning frost covered the ground in front of their cave, and the grasses and shrubs of the forest were tipped with silver. Charlie stood on bare feet before the cave and appeared to be sniffing the air.

"We're gettin' meat today." he said, and passed Sam his Winchester. Sam was not experienced with firearms, though Gus had shown him how to shoot his shotgun once or twice. Sam was not disposed to damping Charlie's recent good mood, and decided not to bring this to his attention. He began picking through his few articles of clothing and putting on all that he owned. He had arrived in the summer, and was not provisioned for winter camping. Within a few minutes

Charlie and Sam had packed for the day, and walked downhill toward the river. The trees were bigger, taller here, and changed from hackberry and cedar elm to oaks and hickories. The ground was littered with acorns. Sunlight streamed into an opening in the woods. Grasses there were tall and dense and covered with frost. Charlie squatted at the base of a water oak and reached, open-palmed, to Sam. Sam carefully placed the Winchester in his hands. The two squatted in the dim light of the forest for an hour. Sam detected a movement at the edge of the clearing. At first he thought it was a bird flitting in the brush, but soon the head of a big doe appeared in the light. She saw them. She stood as still as the trees for minutes. Sam held his breath. Somehow, though he knew he knelt next to him, Charlie was no more animate or human than a tree stump. He had simply disappeared in the vegetation. Slowly, the doe began to relax, and browsed greenbrier along the edge of the clearing. Thunder erupted in Sam's right ear. The doe fell.

Charlie dressed the deer quickly. He pulled strips of sinew off the bone, and cracked the skull open and collected the brains, which he stuffed into the doe's empty bladder. He rolled up the bladder, sinew, backstraps and hams in the skin, tied the ends and draped the bundle across Sam's shoulders. By the time they had returned to camp it was mid-afternoon. Charlie built up the fire and began cutting green saplings, which he fashioned into a rack. He placed the rack and the meat over the fire. The skin he pegged to the ground, and began scraping with a sharp piece of bone he fetched from his gear. He motioned Sam over and handed him the scraper.

"This is gonna be your winter gear, so, you might as well be the one who makes it." said Charlie.

Sam copied Charlie's motions and soon had a good portion of the fat removed. Charlie sat by the fire and poked at the meat with a stick. Little flame reached the meat, but pecan and hickory wood smoke wafted around it. Sam could pay little attention to his task, the smell of melting fat and wood smoke made him unbearably hungry.

Little rain fell as fall moved to winter. For a while, deer searched for forage even at the height of day, making hunting easier, but by late December, Sam and Charlie had taken to fishing the small pools left on the Leon. The fish tasted muddy and nuts gathered in the fall were running short. Rain was finally falling hard on the day that Sam found Charlie kneeling a few yards from the river bank. Water dripped from his long greasy hair. He traced a footprint with his finger.

"A young boar. I saw his print last winter about this time." He followed the track for a few more feet. The bear tracks were no more than a few days old.

"He's fishing around in them old pools, just like we've been. He's hungry, too."

Charlie was silent. He lifted his head and sniffed. No wind blew, and the only sounds were the big drops falling from the bare branches. Charlie climbed down one terrace closer to the stream channel and picked up the trail again. He followed the trail slowly, looking more like a stalking weasel than a man. He placed his feet carefully when he walked. Sam tried to imitate him, but found his feet tangled more often than not, which elicited baleful glares from Charlie.

After a few miles, the bear's trail moved into the brush and upland. Charlie seemed to know where the bear was heading. They walked upstream. The woods became tall and dense enough that they had shaded out the brambles and brush. A thick carpet of last summer's grass lay brown beneath them. Charlie fingered long white scars on a bur oak tree. They were old and healed over. Some bear, maybe the sow he had hunted many years before, had left them. This was the grove, Charlie was sure. He watched the tree tops; he examined the trunks for hair, for scars. There was no indication that a bear had visited recently.

"Maybe he's new to the neighborhood." Sam offered.

"Gettin' dark." Charlie replied.

The sun set long before they made it to camp. Once or twice Charlie paused and felt the moss on the trees. Once satisfied, he moved on with determination. When they arrived, Charlie dragged in some logs and big branches and lit a bonfire. He dragged his old double barreled shot gun out and began to melt down shot, just as he had so many years before. Sam enjoyed the warmth and cheer of the fire, but Charlie seemed more withdrawn than usual. When he had two slugs formed to his satisfaction, he put his tools away, laid down and fell asleep. Sam tried, but it was a waste of a good fire not to enjoy it.

Tree trunks for a full half-acre around were lit by the fire. They stood out white and flat like white paint on black paper. Sam watched the light flicker and wave against the trunks until he began to doze. Staring sleepily into the darkness, Sam noticed a pair of small, marble-sized lights sailing between the trunks. In his doze, the thought they were moths attracted by the flame, though the distance between them didn't change. They were eyes shining in the darkness, Sam realized. He reached toward Charlie to shake him awake, but found him sitting, his shotgun across his lap. He was motionless. In the blackness between the trunks, Sam saw the lights wink out and on again. It was the bear. Though they did not find him, he had had no trouble finding them. The bear chuffed, and then crashed through the thicket, out of the circle of firelight and into the dark. Charlie blew his breath out in a rush, and muttered a few things which Sam didn't understand. The rain picked up again, and in a little while, the fire was out. Sam climbed back into the cave, and slept until Charlie shook him awake.

The morning was wet, and the night's rain heavy enough to have washed the tracks away. However, Charlie knew where he was going — back to the oak grove. It was the best stand, with the richest acorn crop in the area. Charlie took the same circuitous route he had taken before, down to the river, up on the first terrace, watching for tracks and sign as he walked the slow high footed step. Curiously, he had taken only his Winchester, and not the shotgun loaded with slugs. In a few hours, they had made the grove. Charlie found a thicket of rough dogwood and vines and settled on his haunches. He offered Sam some of the venison he had cooked.

He said, "I shot an old sow here back in the 60's. Just after the war. There were still bears and buffalo and panthers around then, but not so many. To find a bear here now, is a stroke of luck. I think this is the last bear on the Leon River." Charlie fell quiet, and then became a stump, as he had when they hunted the doe. Sam dozed, and when he woke, was lying on the ground and covered with leaves. Charlie had likewise covered himself, in a brown lump a few feet away. Sam could hear the thrashing of brush and panting. The bear had arrived. Moving slowly, he parted the leafy cover from one eye and watched as the big boar ripped apart a rotted log, and ate the tasty grubs inside. Rivulets of water ran down his sides without wetting the hair beneath, while ropes of slobber hung from his chin. He was far larger than any of the largest hogs he had seen. His claws were as long as knife blades, but Sam thought his expression was benign. He looked slightly interested in his meal but otherwise bored and a little stupid. Little brown eyes blinked out from the black fur. The bear squatted and relieved himself, and ambled out of the grove, his hips and back swinging through the low brush beyond until he disappeared.

Charlie remained motionless for a few more minutes and took a deep breath. He rose and left the grove. Sam followed. He was confused. Though he had prepared slugs and the bear would have been an easy shot, Charlie had not followed through. For the next several days, they repeated the trip only to bury themselves in leaves and spy. The bear was fat. He would have provided weeks of food. Both Sam and Charlie had gotten thin and the winter was far from over. Sensing Sam's question, one day, Charlie scratched the back of his neck and said, "I suppose, for now, the last bear on the Leon is for admiring."

They returned to the grove daily, and for a week, the bear was absent. In January, snow fell for three days, and they did not venture out of the cave. The little pools on the river had frozen into thick ice. Even the ground itself had frozen hard. Finally, the snow abated one night, and the stars came out. It was the coldest Sam had ever been. Even Charlie seemed uncomfortable, groaning when he turned in his sleep. In the morning the sun, reflected against the snow, lit the inside of the cave like electric light. Little wind blew. The cold had broken.

Sam pulled his blanket around him and crawled blinking, out of the cave and into the blinding light. A soft wind swayed the snow clad branches which dropped their loads in muffled thumps throughout the forest. Charlie climbed out and sniffed the air. He worked his flint to get a little fire started. Soon, they had enough flame to warm themselves. They chewed the last of the jerked meat, along with a few dewberries Sam had dried the previous fall. Charlie had less than what little he usually had to say, and often looked over his shoulder to the north — up river toward the oak grove. After breakfast, he melted snow over the fire in a small frying pan and soaked his beard. He sharpened his knife and hacked through years of matted chin hair. When he finished, his face was not completely hairless, but was uniformly bloody. In the absence of the beard, his eyebrows —already eye-obscuring in their bushiness— were the main feature of his face. He pulled a comb from his pack and began to work through many years of tangles and mats in his hair. Finally, he fashioned it into braids which hung nearly to his waist. He lit a bundle of white sage he had collected in the fall and lit it. He patted and smeared the smoke into his hair and his clothes. He blew a little in Sam's direction too. Charlie packed up his shot gun and his powder and slugs and motioned for Sam to follow.

81

The snow was deep along the river terraces, where it had collected in drifts. The walking was hard, and the snow had begun to melt, soaking through Sam's thin shoes. Charlie maintained a loping gate, lifting his feet almost to his waist, Sam thought. His braids blew in the little bit of breeze and bounced against his back as he bounded. The sun was almost at its height when they neared the grove. Sam saw the back of the bear near the far side of the thicket. The wind was in their favor. He had not detected them. Charlie knelt in the snow and loaded both barrels of the shotgun with slugs. Slowly, they moved forward a few feet at a time, lingering for long minutes, motionless at each stop.

They were now thirty yards from the bear. The wind, which had been gentle at first, began to gust a heavy gray cloud across the sky. The wind subsided; Charlie exhaled, and pulled one trigger. Thunder roared and the bear sat down and groaned. Charlie pulled the second trigger, and the bear fell. Sam's ears rang, but not loud enough to keep out the silence.

Charlie stood, and slowly began the walk to the bear. A rifle shot rang out, and Charlie fell.

"I got you, you no good son-of-a-bitch." The Rocking B cowboy chambered another shell, and hollered for his companions to move up.

BOOK 2

CHAPTER 1

The trial was short. Gus found a Hamilton lawyer who would take on Sam's defense for what little money Gus could gather. The lawyer tossed his hair and hollered and shed real tears over Sam's tender age, but the jury (several were relatives of George Carpenter) sided with the prosecution. For the next six years, the Boy's State School in Gatesville would be his new home. It was not far from Hamilton, but in the four years he would be held there, he would only see Gus twice. Then he came no more. Sam believed him dead, and his suspicion was confirmed when Oscar Biggerstaff joined him at the school. Gus had caught pneumonia, and had died with Mutt attending him only a year after Sam's sentence began. Oscar, who was guilty of the misdemeanor of pushing over one too many outhouses, was awed by Sam's accomplice to murder conviction. The combination of cattle rustling and murder conferred on Sam an aura of respectability which had kept him out of most fights with the other boys. The guards, however, didn't fear him, and beat him for the slightest infraction. The guards were mostly older men. They sweat and swore and wore grey wool uniforms and carried cudgels with which they boxed ears, knocked out eyes and teeth, and caused boys to soil their pants on a regular basis. In winter the boys painted inside of the school. In the spring through the fall they planted, hoed, and picked cotton. July and August were particularly bad. The days were often so hot that even the guards suffered. The heat gave the guards additional ways to punish. Beatings were still regular, but water could be withheld as well. Little boys fell to the dirt with swollen tongues, parched lips, and the whites of their eyes showing. Some were never seen again. Boys ran away, too.

A railroad ran north to south near the school. Sometimes at night, passenger trains passed. Sam stood on the little table in his dormitory. Through a small window, he could see the lights of the passenger cars flash by. Sometimes he could discern features of the riders: A lady's red hat. Someone standing in the aisle. The blur of a face wondering who was there in the darkness. The train came all the way from San Antonio, but more importantly, it headed home. Three older boys managed to hide in boxes of garbage, and made their way past guards and under the fence. The guards knew the railroad track was the road of choice for fleeing boys. In this case, the boys had made five or six miles and ran for the woods when the dogs began to pursue them. The woods were a thicket of greenbrier, and though it slowed the boys, the dogs shied from it. The boys nearly escaped but the oldest one fell into an open well. He was never recovered. The two surviving younger boys lingered a moment too long at the well and were caught. Both were barely recognizable when they were brought in. They spent more than six weeks in isolation. Neither was right again. Sam thought they seemed more compliant though. He guessed that was the point.

In the summer of 1916, Sam and Oscar were permitted to work the cotton field together. The summer was exceptionally wet, and flies and mosquitos were particularly bad. Boys and guards alike were on edge because of the added nuisance. Oscar rubbed guards the wrong way from the beginning. It was his nature, though he was never

84

outwardly defiant. Oscar felt he was a greater intellect than most at the school —especially guards and other authorities— and believed he could insult them with his sharp wit without the dullards knowing they had been knifed. One fly-infested July day, Oscar asked for water from a guard who had been hard on him for most of the afternoon. The guard snarled that water was for those who worked.

Oscar offered, "The fact that I just seen you slurp a big dipperful is evidence to the contrary."

Though it took the guard a moment, his face turned red and he showed Oscar his teeth. His fury was such that he was unable to speak. He reached for his cudgel. Oscar ran. Four guards tackled him, and the offended guard straddled him while the others pinned Oscar's arms and legs down. He beat Oscar's face with the cudgel till Oscar no longer struggled. Flies were already at the blood on him. The field was silent, though one hundred boys and fifteen guards were in a tight bunch. The fury of the guards subsided, and the wielder of the cudgel looked up, open-mouthed; surprised at the attention. Oscar was bundled in a sheet and taken away. Sam's ears buzzed and he couldn't think. He didn't want to think. Oscar had always been capable. Nothing could stop him, but he had been stopped.

The boys were brought in from the field early, and locked in the dormitory without the customary supper. Sam stood on a table and watched the sky. Ugly black clouds, tinged with green, boiled in southwest. The muggy air was still and electric with anticipation. Not long after sunset, thunder rumbled and Sam, still at the window, watched chain lightning that played on the horizon in flashes so constant and so close together that they looked like a curtain of light. Hail stones the size of hen's eggs pounded the dormitory roof. The few bare bulbs providing light flickered, and then went out. The wind screamed under the eaves of the metal roof, which first popped and flexed, and then began to show light where it joined the walls. Sam held his hands to his ears as the suction which made them pop took the roof off into the night sky. Its flight was bird-like: flapping and silhouetted by lightning until it grew small and disappeared.

For a moment, Sam stood admiring the night sky. The tornado had made a deafening roar, but now it was so quiet, he could hear his own breath. Within a few seconds, the stillness was broken by shouts and screams. A boy lay with part of his leg gone. Some boys walked, stunned; their faces covered in blood. A number of boys were missing. Sam made no plan. His legs just carried him to the window, now void of bars and ceiling. He climbed down to the wet ground and crouched, listening. The storm had passed and the lightning flashed in the blackness far from the school. Other dormitories appeared intact, but one guard hut was reduced to sticks. Another had been picked up and dumped on the perimeter fence, collapsing almost three hundred feet of barbed wire. Sam ran.

The sun rose clear. Sam slept with his back against the creek bank. A chattering squirrel woke him, and it took him a moment to realize where he was and how he had gotten there. He peered over the bank. The pasture east was littered with debris. He guessed he was at least four miles from the school. The little creek he had followed had started as a gully in the pasture next to the school farm. Old cans and pieces of cookstove and iron farm implements were dumped in the gully head to arrest erosion. A sharp piece had ripped his calf, and he inspected the cut. It was deep, though he thought the rain had washed out most of the dirt. He made a poultice of moss and wrapped it in rag. He believed he was not far from the highway. He would make Fort Worth. He would get away.

CHAPTER 2

The remaining guards made head counts three times. The first was within minutes of Sam's escape. The dead and dying were tallied and taken away. The living were counted and moved into less damaged housing. The five missing boys were hunted. Two were found dead, one impaled on a tree limb. Dogs were used to search for the others, but to little effect. Rain had washed away the scent, and the authorities suspected their remains, too, would show up eventually. Within a week, Sam, along with the others, was counted as a casualty.

Sam had managed to find clothes blown from someone's wash line. Overalls and a ragged white shirt made him look like anyone else's skinny kid out to seek his fortune, and that is what Sam had decided. It was time for him to be someone else. He liked the idea of being someone luckier. He had heard that there might be a job in the stockyards. Sam Wood might not be lucky enough to land one, but 'Sam Cook' was.

Sam smelled Fort Worth long before he saw it. He had heard that the stock yards could yield a powerful smell. It was nightfall by the time he made them. He had made the trip in three rides, and the last was in the back of a truck loaded with pigs. Two or three lights shown from the little offices scattered between the holding pens. Though he held little hope, Sam knocked on a door. A young man with a cigarette stuck to his lower lip shoved his head out the door and into Sam's face.

"What can I do fer ya kiddo? Want some candy? Ain't Halloween, yet!" He laughed, and motioned for Sam to come in.

Sam hid his hurt hand in his pocket. The room was rank with the smell of tobacco spit, smoke, and cowshit.

"I bet you run away from home, and now you think you're gonna make a fortune shovelin' manure?" he mused. "Well, been that way forever, and I am glad to provide you with a shovel. You can make ten cents a day, and if that works out, we can find somethin' else for you to do. What's yer name?"

"Sam Cook." he replied, unable to believe his luck.

"Well Sam Cook, if you have no place to sleep, you are welcome to find some clean hay and bed down. Come see me in the morning. My name is Ed Wright, and I am night foreman for this end of the Armour outfit."

There was more than enough clean hay in the loft above the pens. Sam lay on his back in the soft hay and had almost fallen asleep when he remembered George Carpenter's shed and the rat run. He investigated the pile for rodents, but found no sign. He assumed the hay was pitched too frequently for rats to get too comfortable. True to his word, Ed Wright showed up in the morning with a big grain scoop and handed it to Sam. Sam reached out to take it with his incomplete hand.

"God almighty, kid ...what happened to you?" Ed asked, as he took a step back.

"Rattlesnake." replied Sam, and took the shovel. "It don't matter. I can shovel, write ...pick my nose. It's no trouble."

90

Ed grinned. "Well I be damned, if you ain't a tomcat." Ed gave Sam a biscuit with a little greasy sausage in it. The day was begun.

There was a wagon with tall sides in the first pen he worked in. On its floor lay a covering of hay. The cattle, mainly calves and long yearlings, had been moved to an adjacent pen while he played chamber maid. The tornado at Gatesville had just been a big rain at the stockyards. The cow flop was mostly water and was churned up into slurry. After a few tries, he discovered that he could fill a shovel by driving the flop across the pen and making windrows. At the end of each run, he had enough solid matter collected in the shovel to pitch into the cart. The flies and stench were bad, and his Boy's School shoes were ruined, but he persisted until five pens were cleaned. Compared to cotton farming at the school, the job was pleasant. No guards oversaw or hollered at him or beat him. In fact, no one interrupted him until the end of the day. Ed looked him over.

"You are one sorry sight. If them clothes are all you got, I got a spare pair of overhauls I can lend." He scratched his chin thoughtfully. "There's a place in the yards that sells old clothes. At the end of the week you'll have half a dollar or so. You can get you some spares."

Sam alternated his with Ed's clothes for the remainder of the week, and washed the shit-caked clothes in a water trough. Sam noted that the cows did not shy from the soup he made each night, but often drank while he scrubbed. On Saturday, Sam got fifty cents and a dollar advance to cover his expenses. He was one of the few boys who was not only adept at shoveling manure, but was pleased to do it. He walked from the yards down Main Street with Ed, who turned out to be only two years older. The sun shone on the red tile of the Stock Exchange building. It was the biggest building Sam had ever seen. There were fine hotels, and not-so-fine hotels. There were saloons and eateries; saddle shops and mercantiles. There was much to entertain if one had money. Sam held his tight in his fist inside his pocket. A new, or at least intact, pair of shoes was his greatest ambition. The leather of his shoes had gone stiff and cracked with the constant wetness. The toes of his left foot wiggled in cow dung as he worked. The little shop that sold old clothes was not far. Sam thought it must cater specifically to pen shovelers — the need was so great.

Afterward, Sam and Ed sat on the edge of the street as Ed rolled a cigarette.

"You know, you ought ta smoke to keep down the smell of those boogers. Let me roll you one. I'll show ya how." He pulled out a little cheesecloth bag of tobacco, and crinkled up two cigarette papers. "Ya wad 'em up first. Makes 'em easier that way." He rolled the cigarettes with one hand. He was showing off. After Ed lit them, Sam took a long drag and coughed and retched.

"That's good smoke!" he exclaimed after he had regained his composure. Sam felt on top of the world, though a bit whirly.

"Looky here." said Ed. He took a long drag and looked at Sam earnestly. "I ain't gonna work in the yard much longer. Me and some other fellers are joinin' the National Guard. We heard the Mexicans are causin' trouble in South Texas, even killin' some folks, and we're gonna go help out." Ed went on to explain that he and the boys would go down to Fort Bliss in El Paso, get uniforms, three meals a day and a decent place to sleep.

"Would be better than smellin' cow shit all day, and we might get to shoot some Mexicans." Ed slapped Sam on the back. "You oughta go, too. Better than shovelin' that stuff."

Sam pulled his bad hand out of his pocket. "Think they'll take me with this?"

Ed appraised Sam's hand. "Army might not, but I bet the Guard will. Can you shoot?"

"Sure can." said Sam. He wasn't sure, but the trip sounded like a good idea. He wasn't sure how old you had to be, but Sam Cook would be old enough. He was getting used to a fib now and then, if it served a good purpose. Ed talked Sam into eating at a little shack, where a Mexican woman made tamales. Though they cost Sam almost a half day of wages, they were the best thing Sam had ever eaten.

"If goin' down to Mexico means I get to eat these things every day, I am goin' tomorrow."

Ed's friends found them leaning against the wall picking their teeth. "Let's go." said one with ears that stood out from his head like bat wings. "If we wait, I'm gonna change my mind."

The five of them walked the three miles to the recruiter, which was in a nicer part of the city. It was not too nice, but it did not smell of cow. Sam was last to sign his papers. He decided to let the recruiter notice his hand, rather than announce it.

"Can you shoot with that thing?" The recruiter squinted at his hand.

"You bet," he grinned. "I used to win turkey shoots, but I'm a little rusty ... It don't hold me back." Sam said with more confidence than he felt. The recruiter decided Sam could be put to some use on the border. He would let them decide when he got there.

CHAPTER 3

A few weeks passed before the boys had to report to the train station for the long trip to Fort Bliss. Sam had never ridden a train. He thought about those he had seen when he had been in Gatesville: the hiss of steam, the rumble of the tremendous weight as it passed by, the lucky and exotic passengers barely visible as the train shot past. Sam jumped when his train shot a jet of steam that sounded part like a snake and partly like a gunshot. The boys laughed at him, but Ed was sympathetic. "You'll have to get used to loud noise. I reckon we're about to hear a lot of it." He looked grave, and gave Sam a hard candy and patted him on the head. His face then broke into a grin and he snickered. "Yeehaw!! We are gonna have a time of it!!" He slapped Sam on the back.

The train car was full of young men and old boys. There were some in fine suits and others, like him, in worn overalls. Shaving cuts and pimples were abundant. The smell of sweat and hair tonic made the summer heat in the close car worse. Sam and Ed sat together on a hard seat. Ed reached across Sam, who sat by the window, and after some fiddling managed to open the window. A thick pall of smoke and cinders choked them before Ed could get the window closed again. The car jerked, once, then twice and the train began to roll. Sam watched the train station roll pass. He felt like he did the day he and Gus had ridden out of Hamilton for Fairy, high above the lesser crowds, princely in this novel form of conveyance.

West of Fort Worth, the land stretched out and rolled in waves as far as Sam could see. It looked like the Rocking B, but it had no little wooded valleys, or cedar-clad bluffs, just grass as far as he could see. A cowboy galloped his horse alongside the train and whooped and beat his horse with his hat, but the train outdistanced him. The boys in the car all crowded to the windows, and the car pitched precariously to one side. The springs held, though, and all remained long enough to see the horseman disappear into the distance. Ed whispered, "You'd think they'd a seen enough cowboys in Fort Worth to last 'em for a while, though those were usually drunk and not doin' any cowboyin'." Sam was no exception. He craned his neck out of the window, and when the cowboy vanished he could see the engine ahead as it turned slightly north. In late afternoon, the land became broken and covered in scrubby oaks. The soil was red and gold. The setting sun made the leaves of the oaks shine, and the air smelled dry and dusty. A steward came and lit oil lamps in the car. Sam pulled open a sack with some biscuits and boiled eggs, and some hard candy he had bought at the train station. He and Ed ate silently as the night sky blazed stars and the train ate up the miles.

Over the next two days, the land became flatter. Oaks were replaced by mesquite and then by scrubby brush and weeds Sam did not know. Dust and sand seeped into all the crevices in Sam's skin that soot and cinders did not already occupy. When the train rolled to a stop in El Paso, he saw several soldiers standing at the landing, while others who looked like they might be officers, were mounted on horses.

A Sergeant with a red and sweaty face blew a whistle and corralled the recruits onto the landing, and hollered at them a number of things which Sam could not understand. He was tired and hungry and the smell of tamales from a little vending cart wafted past his nose. A fly crawled across his cheek, but he was too scared of the Sergeant to wiggle much. After the first batch of hollering was over, the Sergeant consulted a mounted officer and the second batch began. The recruits, who numbered more than fifty, were marched directly south, down the tracks to Fort Bliss. Sam had reasonably good work boots on, but many of the recruits had thin-soled fancy shoes, and the gravel and rocks along the rail bed hurt their feet. Sam had only a paper bag to hold his belongings, though many recruits dragged suitcases along. Sam stepped over the abandoned luggage that had been dropped after the second mile.

Late in the afternoon, they arrived at a flat piece of ground next to the rail. The mountains cast a little shadow on the flats and made it slightly cooler. Little dirty tents shaped like those used in the circus covered a hundred acres or more. The wind whipped between them and stirred up little spumes of dust. What little grass that had been there when the camp was made had long been trampled to dirt. The men and boys were herded to one of the larger tents, where they were given boots, underwear and uniforms. After he was assigned a tent mate —no one he knew— and was yelled at and herded to his tent, he placed his civilian clothes in his paper bag and emerged a soldier, though his gaiters drooped. The recruits were inspected, barked at, and told to line up for chow. Sam thought the food some of the best he had ever eaten. There was beef, and two kinds of vegetables, and best of all, white bread. Sam had not eaten white bread since living with Mutt. Corn bread and corn dodgers and corn mush made up most of what he was fed or could scrounge in the past few years.

In the morning, the recruits were fed again, and then herded into a large hall. A couple of Iowa boys mooed like cows and bleated like sheep until a Sergeant ran over and hollered in their faces. A captain explained that their training was to begin that very morning. Each man would be assigned to a platoon, led by a Drill Sergeant. Marching, marksmanship, and physical training would be their lives for the next few weeks. Sam was assigned to a platoon made up of country boys. The two boys who had mooed and bleated were present. Most of the recruits were from Texas, but a few of the others were from Kansas and one was from Arkansas. Animal imitation continued to be a popular past time. In the mornings, the Iowa boys crowed like roosters and the Arkansan grunted like a pig. By the end of the week, the Texans had taken up their favorite livestock noises, and the camp sounded like a barnyard. The routine of drill, physical exercise, rifle range, and three meals each day suited Sam. It was the regularity he admired. He didn't worry about what would happen next. Someone had already planned next for him.

The winter came on without word of much fighting along the border. Sam's hand had finally caught the attention of his Drill Sergeant, who determined him unfit for the field, and he moved between mess duty and the hospital as need arose. The winter was the coldest Sam could remember. He assumed Fort Bliss, being close to the deserts of Mexico, would be warm in winter, but little snow squalls were common by January. He awoke many mornings with a dusting of snow on his blanket. However, biscuits and butter and coffee were abundant and made the cold dry days bearable. After some weeks of emptying bedpans and changing sheets, Sam was given the job assisting nurses with taking vitals and occasionally changing dressings on the few wounds. There were no battle wounds yet, but there were more than a few ingrown toenails from ill-fitted boots, and broken bones from mishaps with mules and equipment. One of the nurses, a girl from Illinois, took an interest in Sam, especially his injured hand. She listened with rapt attention to the story of his snakebite, which Sam embellished as to the snake's size and his own bravery. Her interest was in part professional. Poisonous snakes were few in her home country, and they —especially rattlesnakes— were abundant in southwest Texas. They also came in many different shapes and forms here. Sam basked in her attention and he soon became smitten with Katherine. She was a small woman, a little older than Sam, with a round pale face and eyes so large she always appeared a little surprised. Her hair was dark; almost black, and she had a little bow of a mouth. Sam, being new to these feelings, tried always to impress her, and though he was still a gawky boy, she appreciated his efforts and encouraged his attention.

Katherine's interest extended to Sam's training as well. As he became more proficient at nursing, the demand for his services rose and he was relieved of most of his mess duties.

By April, he was performing most of the duties of the regular nurses. The spring around El Paso was a dry time, though little thunderstorms occasionally rose over the mountains. Sam appreciated the smell of even distant moisture, and he imagined his dry nose and lungs absorbing the goodness of it. Sunsets behind thunderstorms were green and magenta and purple. Sam and 'Kate,' as he had come to call her, watched the colors fade until night overtook the mountains. The moonlight lit the mountains like day, and the silence of the desert on such nights made Sam's ears buzz. One warm April night, Sam held Kate as they lay together on his scratchy wool blanket. Their peace was broken by shouts in camp, as an officer's car and a motorcycle pulled up to the hospital.

"Mr. Villa has sacked Columbus, right across the border." an officer hollered. "We got the best of the son-of-a-bitch, though. We still have casualties and we need to get the worst ones back to this hospital." Sam volunteered for ambulance duty. There were four mule-drawn ambulances and one new Dodge panel truck. Sam was assigned to one of the former to assist the driver and stretcher bearer. The moonlight, which had been romantic, was now essential to their getting across the low mountains and into the New Mexican desert. The sun was rising as they rolled into Columbus. Several buildings still burned and a few were just heaps of smoldering wood and adobe. The Mexican dead were many. Laid side by side, two rows spanned the town's main street. The American dead were relatively few, but there were wounded. A small hospital was established at a brick school building, the largest in town. By the time Sam and his crew arrived, the badly wounded were being loaded onto the motor-ambulance, which could carry six, stacked one over the other like loaves of bread on oven racks. Little rivers of blood trickled from the floor of the ambulance onto the dusty street. Sam swooned momentarily; then pressed on with folded stretcher in hand. The wounded lay on the school's floor and nurses and a doctor tried to staunch bleeding on the struggling and comfort the dying. Sam lifted the shoulders of a man so bloody that he could not distinguish his features. He howled and cursed as he was moved.

"We're gonna take you back to Bliss, where you can get better." Sam said, not knowing what other comfort he could give.

The man laughed through his pain, and said, "I could use a little bliss, right now, got any?" Sam smiled and asked if he could roll him a cigarette. He lit it for him and held it to the man's lips until he had taken a decent drag. The man lost consciousness and the bearers took him to the ambulance.

Sam moved to a man who had lost most of the right side of his face. He was conscious though, and was whispering to a nurse who looked at Sam and shook her head sadly. "I don't know if he will live through the trip to El Paso, but we can't treat him here." she whispered between clenched teeth. Sam knelt next to him and asked him if he needed anything before they put him on the ambulance. "Sam" he whispered, and turned his remaining eye to Sam's face. Ed reached out for Sam's hand.

"I'm gonna take good care of you, Ed. Better than what the rest get, because you are my good friend. Besides, we got to get back to Fort Worth and poke cattle, girls, and eat those good tamales." He talked the stretcher bearer into moving another man down, so Ed could have the top stretcher. He had already seen that the lower ones were getting covered up in the blood dripping from the top. It was night when the ambulance arrived at the hospital.

CHAPTER 4

Ed was alive, but unconscious. Sam wanted to linger a bit until Ed was settled in, but the driver was at his elbow at an instant. "We got one more load to bring in, and the moon is goin' ta set in a few hours. Let's git!" Sam sat in the back of the ambulance. Tears of grief ran down his face for Ed and for the shock of seeing so much blood and pain. Sam thought it was easier to bear one's own pain than carry such a load of the pain of others. After a few miles he fell asleep and awoke to shouting. It was in Spanish.

Sam climbed out of the ambulance and was struck down by the butt of a rifle. The driver and stretcher bearer were still on the wagon and once he regained his feet, he climbed to the seat and squeezed in next to the stretcher bearer. Though he could not understand Spanish, he got the gist that they were to follow the seven horsemen south. There was no road or trail, and when the wagon soon stuck crossing the river, the Mexicans took the harnesses off the mules and motioned for them to mount. Sam struggled over the mule's haunches and sat behind the ambulance driver. His head throbbed from the thumping he had received. The mules were not accustomed to riders, and the stretcher bearer was soon thrown from his. The Mexicans paused for a moment to discuss the lack of transportation. One drew his pistol, but another stayed his hand. They decided to let the stretcher bearer wander back to Texas if he could find his way.

After a few hours, the moon set, and Sam could see the little bit shown in the starlight. Their mule was cooperative, and Sam wished he had been the one bucked off and set free. His head hurt, and the mule's backbone was so sharp and his gait so uneven that he thought he would be lucky to have a butt or his privates left by the time they got to wherever it was they were going.

The driver whispered to Sam, "I think they're goin' ta ransom us. That's why they let Bill go — to tell 'em what happened."

"No talking!!" shouted one the Mexicans in English.

A gray smear of light appeared to Sam's left. They were still going south, and the earth began to release its morning smell. He could smell damp sheep droppings, so he knew they were coming to somewhere settled. They crested a hill, and in a shallow valley lay a little adobe house. A Model T Ford was parked in the door yard, and several men hunkered around a little fire there. The men at the fire rose and watched the band of horsemen descend the hill. There was a stronger smell of sheep mixed with the good smells of coffee and wood smoke. The men around the fire stood and picked up their rifles, though they only watched. When the group entered the camp, the driver and Sam were pulled from their horses and escorted to the fire. The demeanor of their captors surprised them. They were polite to the point of being cordial, and once their captives were seated, brought them sweet coffee and tortillas. Sam was scared, but it had been a long time since he had eaten.

"You are prisoners of General Villa." explained a tall man in a dusty black frock coat. His hair was slicked down and parted in the middle. He wore pince-nez glasses and a neatly trimmed goatee. His English was good and his accent sounded like south Texas. "I am Dr. Gomez Najera, and I am your host." He bowed slightly. "Our friends here will not harm you, as long as you do not try to escape." he smiled. "Even now, we are arranging with the Americans for your release. Enjoy your breakfast, gentlemen. Get some sleep and we will talk later." Sam and his driver, who had whispered that his name was Owens, were led to the house. A little fire burned in one corner, and Sam and Owens made their beds on a pile of dirty blankets in the other.

When Sam awoke, the sun was low on the horizon, and the Mexicans were in the house. A few of them wore fancy boots and spurs and bandoliers of bullets across their chests. Most, however, just looked like the ranch hands and cowboys Sam was accustomed to seeing. Dr. Najera was there as well. "I hope you rested well." he said. "Our accommodations are rustic, but I am sure you are raw-boned American boys." An old man with few teeth smiled as he brought Sam and Owens cups of coffee so sweet it made Sam's teeth ache.

Sam looked at Najera and said, "You speak English as good as we do. Maybe better." Najera laughed and pulled on his beard.

"I am from San Antonio, you see. My mother was a chambermaid for a rich gringa. The old lady took a shine to me. She thought I was the smartest little brown boy she had seen. So ..." he sighed. "She took up my training and with her connections she was able to get me into Yale University in the east, I was the only little brown boy there." Najera picked at a fingernail. "I became a medical doctor. Because those of my race can only treat their own kind, I had many patients but little money. I could have gone into poultry farming, though!" He smiled. "I was paid in chickens,

105

sometimes corn meal, tortillas; a goat or two. I saw what was happening in the country of my mother's birth, and it appeared that the brown people were treated here the same as they were in San Antonio." He stood and his look was severe. "This will not stand. I am Mexican now, a Villista, and this is a revolution in my own country for the rights of the Indians, the brown people, the farmers, the dispossessed!" He strode to a cabinet in the corner of the little hut, and pulled out a dusty canvas bag. "This is why you're here!" He dumped the contents, which looked like Mexican money. "We have been minting this for years in San Antonio. We are rich in fiat currency, but our creditors require something a bit more solid. That is hard American cash. You will help us get it so that we can continue to shoot at you, and anyone else who needs to be shot at." He laughed so hard he coughed for a while. "Ironic, don't you think?"

Sam thought Dr. Najera was one of those people who laughed when he was angry. Out of nervousness, he had laughed when Najera laughed like it was all a joke. However, he did not see the irony in his situation, nor was he sure what ironic meant, anyway. Gomez Najera left the hut, and talked to some men outside. The old man returned with hot tortillas. Days passed. Though Sam and Owens were not tied, they were confined to the little room. The routine remained the same: coffee and tortillas in the early morning; a trip to the bushes to relieve themselves at mid-morning; sitting on the blankets until night; beans, tortillas and more coffee when the sun went down. Najera frequently returned and talked to them cordially. He occasionally acted as physician and assessed their health by inspecting their eyes and looking into their mouths.

Mostly, Sam thought of Kate. He remembered the flash of her eyes and the touch of her hand. He thought of her kisses. She was the first girl he had kissed. Her breath reminded him of plums, it was so sweet. Though the Mexicans had not been cruel, he feared he would never see her again.

One warm night in the second week of their captivity, a Mexican rolled a cigarette and offered it to Sam. Sam seldom smoked, but the activity would break the boredom. The tobacco had a strange herbal taste, but Sam assumed it was the way Mexican tobacco should taste. Other men in the room watched Sam smoke. Their eyes shined and they smiled and chuckled as he coughed. One of the older men bent to ladle a dipper of beans onto his plate. He passed gas so forcefully that Sam thought he saw the little curtain on the door flutter. Another farted in response. All the men were silent, smiling, and staring at Sam, who could not stifle a chuckle which rose to a belly laugh that he could not stop. He rolled on the floor laughing. Owens glared in disapproval. Pretty soon all but Owens were rolling on the floor with laughter.

At Fort Bliss, a red-faced Colonel had received orders to rescue the kidnapped ambulance men. After consultation among Generals and Congressmen, it was determined that payment of ransom was out of the question. It would set a precedent which could haunt the country for the remainder of the conflict. Instead, the red-faced Colonel assembled an expedition into Mexico. An Apache tracker was found in southern New Mexico, and a unit of cavalry assembled. The Colonel, unable to find motorized transportation to his liking, outfitted his Dodge touring car with a driver, tent, and an ornate coffee urn for the expedition. Kate assembled a kit of bandages and tape and enclosed a letter for Sam. She imposed on a young private to deliver it. Since his disappearance, she had slept little, though the new hope of his rescue revived her some. The rescue party left Fort Bliss the morning of Sam's laughing fit. The sun was red on the horizon when they left, and their dust showed pink as they headed for the Rio Grande. Sam was different than the boys she had known in Illinois. He was rough, but there was sweetness and a lack of guile in him that she loved. She remembered his kisses and she missed him.

The Mexicans hauled Owens and Sam to the campfire, where they lit several more cigarettes. A guitar was brought from the hut, and the group began to sing. Sam enjoyed the music, and though he could not understand the words, he knew they were about pain and humor and love and the word "Corazon" was common. He reached to accept the cigarette from a tall smiling Mexican who suddenly fell backwards onto the campfire. Another bullet ricocheted on the ground in front of Sam who lay cringing; face down. Owens had run for the brush. The Mexicans sporadically returned fire. The ground was lit by muzzle flashes. When he lifted his head slightly, he could see the flash of rifle fire from the brush at the edge of the clearing. He heard horse hooves and looked to see a dozen cavalry dash into the clearing, driving the Mexicans into the chaparral. Sam stood and raised his hands in surrender. Owens was dragged from hiding in the brush.

The red-faced Colonel demanded, "Are you Americans?"

"Yesser, I am a Texan," shouted Sam, "but I don't know where Owens is from." Sam and Owens were shoved into the back of the touring car.

The Colonel growled, "You idiots have cost us time and inconvenience. We'll leave you to 'em if this happens again." Sam thought that might not be such a bad thing. He wished he could get more of those cigarettes. He felt sorry for the smiling man who died handing him one. He wondered what had become of Najera. A cavalryman had passed a letter to Sam through the car's window. Sam stuffed it in his blouse pocket to read in private later. He recognized Kate's writing.

CHAPTER 5

Sam was surprised how close the border was. The journey on mule-back had taken all night. The touring car made it back in a few hours. The red-faced Colonel escorted Owens and Sam to an equally red brick building on the base. Sam had seen it at some distance, but had never been inside. It was different than the other canvas and mud architecture about the camp. It looked like a house George Washington might have lived in, it was so grand. The door was guarded by two soldiers, who saluted the Colonel stiffly as he approached. Inside, a long corridor led to an office with a very stiff mustachioed General at a big desk. He was surrounded by, and giving orders to, lesser officers who dashed this way then that, when he barked at them. Sam could tell that most of the men in the room were afraid of him. Sam was afraid, too. The Colonel stood silently at attention waiting for the General's permission to speak.

The general glared at the Colonel and said, "Jake, give your report to my adjutant and leave these sons-of-bitches to me."

"Yes, General Pershing, sir!" He saluted and exited the room quickly. The General sent the other officers scurrying, and when the room was empty, he tented his fingers and glared at Sam, and then Owens. He spent some time in this activity, alternating between the two. In part, he seemed to be sizing them up, but at the same time, he appeared to attempt some physical injury with his eyes.

Once the staring ritual had concluded, the General said, "You two miscreants have caused some trouble. Your job was to deliver wounded from Columbus to Fort Bliss, but instead, you decided to entertain the goddamned Villistas, who sought fifteen thousand hard earned American dollars for your release. Of course, the nation is not responsible for buying your worthless carcasses, so we instead sent twenty-five of our finest cavalry, not to mention a bird Colonel to rescue you. Your inability to conduct business put almost thirty lives at risk. The final straw is that we now have not only two Texas newspapers seeking interviews, but the Washington Post as well." He resumed staring and then rose to pace the floor; his hands were clasped behind his back. "These are your orders. I have prepared a list of acceptable questions and your answers to those questions. You will meet the press in the company of your unit's commanding officer. You will be considered some kind of ... folk heroes who have suffered but survived the ordeal of capture by a deranged and dangerous enemy. You will be returned to your units and placed on limited duty." The following day, Owen and Sam would meet with the General's adjutant, who would give them further instructions.

Sam had almost forgotten the letter in his pocket. He decided to have Kate read it to him, and found her at the hospital, cleaning bed pans.

He stood behind her until she turned. "I thought you saved those things for me." he smiled. Kate's eyes brimmed with tears. She reached for him but reconsidered, given the public setting.

"Oh, Sam, I am so glad ...come see me at my barracks tonight." her voice trembled. She looked at the floor and then through her brow at him. "And bring a blanket." she whispered.

After he and Owens met with the General's adjutant, who rehearsed them in answering questions, Sam tapped on the window of Kate's barrack. A horse-faced woman opened the window and scowled at him. A few minutes later Kate came to the window and, bending at the waist, leaned out to kiss him.

"Did you bring the blanket?"

"Yessum." replied Sam, who dug his toe into the dirt.

The sun was beginning to set when they finally arranged the blanket at the foot of a little hill behind the nurse's barracks. Kate smoothed and re-smoothed the blanket, and tugged at the corners.

"How is Ed?" asked Sam. Sam thought Kate's attention to the blanket might be avoidance of the topic.

"Ed was moved to Waco." she frowned. "He will live, but his face is so disfigured, Sam. They can help him some, and there are prostheses they can make for him, too."

Sam shifted on the blanket. "Well, that is mostly good news, I suppose. What is prostheses?" Kate looked away at the blanket again.

"They can build something like a mask ...to cover the missing parts. It will make it easier for him when he is in public." Sam rolled a cigarette and noticed the failing light.

"I'm goin' to see him in Waco, then. Maybe I can cheer him up."

He pulled the letter from his breast pocket. The light was beginning to get a little pink and shadowy, and he wanted Kate to read the letter before it failed. "I've not read this, yet." He passed the letter to Kate. "Read it to me?" Kate smiled and opened an end of the envelope and shook it till the paper fell out. She unfolded it and read:

"Sam —

If you read this letter it will mean that you have survived your ordeal with the Mexicans. What joy, that I will see you again! The prospect of your safe return is the only thing which has kept me going in the past few sleepless weeks. I am fond of you, Sam, and I had no idea that my fondness would grow to love until I faced losing you forever. I love you Sam, and I want you by my side. I can say no more, for those few words are profound enough in themselves."

Kate's gaze slowly rose to Sam's eyes. Neither spoke. Sam pulled a handkerchief from his seat pocket and blew his nose. He was crying, though he did not want Kate to know.

CHAPTER 6

A large white tent was erected for the newspaper men. It was open on the sides and the wind blew bits of paper from the tables. Sam and Owens sat on camp stools in the middle; the red-faced Colonel and the General's adjutant stood behind them. The reporters sat in a semi-circle around. Sam's palms sweated and his heart pounded in his chest. He was asked how he was treated: "Terribly." How was he fed? "Poorly." Was he glad to be home? Emphatically, "Yes." A few cameras flashed and his picture was taken, shaking the hand of the red-faced Colonel. A reporter shouted, "Hey, son, how'd ya lose your hand?" The adjutant informed the awed crowd that Sam had been tortured by the Mexicans, but through true American strength and grit, had not revealed any military secrets to the barbarians. Sam's good hand was shaken repeatedly, and his back was slapped so many times he was sure it had hand prints. The red-faced Colonel even shook hands with Sam again.

"Looks like you're a hero, boy." the Colonel grinned. Sam did not know what to say. The story was official, and he did not want to cross General Pershing. Sam Wood had lost his hand to a rattlesnake, but Sam Cook's was taken by the Mexicans while he was being a hero.

Sam told Kate, who was a little offended, but not surprised. She thought the military would do what was necessary to win the war, and if a good tale helped the cause, Sam should be for it. When Sam thought of it that way, it seemed a bit less of a lie. It wasn't his lie, anyway. He hadn't told it.

When the Colonel found Sam the next day, he was sitting under a window of the hospital, waiting for Kate to peer out. He was so smitten, he peeked in from time to time and wiggled his fingers at her. When she smiled, he snorted and hid again. The Colonel grabbed Sam's shoulder in the act of this peek-a-boo, and informed him that he should pack immediately and meet a driver who would take him to the train depot. Sam thought the Colonel's face expressed only one emotion, regardless of that which he might wish to express. Did he pitch woo, Sam wondered, with a red, sweaty face, bulging eyes, and clenched teeth? Before he packed, Sam wrote a short letter to Ed and gave it to Kate to mail.

"I'm going to miss you." he said.

Kate kissed Sam on the cheek and said, "Write to me, Sam. Write to me so I know you haven't forgot me."

A young officer accompanied him to the train, and informed him he was to participate in a parade in Fort Worth. He was considered a wounded hero, and the folks there wanted to look at him. The young officer —a second lieutenant named Murphy— was to accompany him to make sure he did nothing to embarrass the army. The train pulled out into the desert at sunset, and as Sam had taken a seat on the west side of the car, he had a fine view of the same sunset he had shared with Kate, who occupied all of his thoughts now. He had found that eye gazing with Kate had transported him beyond anything he had ever experienced. Her lips were dry, due to the climate, but behind them, her sweet mouth had been like honey.

The wind blew hard from the south, and the smoke and cinders were not as much of a problem on the north bound train. When he woke in the morning, the land had turned from red clay and sand to limestone. A misty rain wet the cedars on the hills and bluffs and gave the air a sweet aroma that made him homesick; made him think of Billy and Mutt and Gus. After two more days, they entered the prairie country southwest of Fort Worth. The wind was still southerly, and Sam could not make out the smell of the stockyards. The city could be seen from miles away, and a little pall of smoke hovered over it like an umbrella. The train arrived at the platform and Sam and Murphy were greeted by a party of old women in fancy hats, some wearing silk sashes across their torsos. They were representatives of the Daughters of the Confederacy. They shook Sam's good hand and tried not to look at the other. They had arranged for a motor car to drive them to a hotel. Sam had never spent the night in a hotel, and as it turned out, neither had Murphy, who was a nice enough fella for an officer. A suite had been arranged for the soldiers at the Stockyards Hotel. Sam could not believe his luck. "I used to work just down the street from there!" he shouted at Murphy over the roar of the car engine. As they pulled up the street, his thoughts turned to Ed. He suddenly felt so sorry that he had not been able to go with him to Waco, it nearly soured his excitement.

Sam and his entourage pulled to the curb in front of the hotel. They entered the lobby, decorated with huge paintings and a chandelier. The ceilings looked as high as the sky. What little luggage Sam had was scooped up by a uniformed attendant, and he and Murphy were led to an elevator, a new experience for them both. There were two adjoining rooms, paid for by the Daughters, with feather beds and heavy drapes and a fancy carpet on the floor. A desk with hotel stationery was in the corner. Sam could not believe the luxury. However, he was compelled to write Kate, to let her know he had arrived and to tell her how much he missed her. Murphy had a girlfriend in Fort Worth, and he left soon after their arrival, leaving Sam on his own.

> "Dear Kate," he wrote, "We got to Fort Worth at four o'clock this afternoon and are at the Stockyard Hotel. It is fancier than I can tell. I wished you were here. I miss you and miss Ed, too. Hope you are well and can write me soon."

> Best wishes,

> Sam Cook

The sun was going down behind the hotel when he got to the street, which had electric lamps making it like daylight, he thought. Sam walked to the cattle pens, and was overwhelmed by their familiar smell. Going to work in the pens had been the beginning of a better life for him, and he associated the smell with it. Tears came to his eyes, though he wasn't sure if it was sentimentality or manure vapors that caused it. Sam realized he was in his dress uniform, and it wouldn't do to soil it with manure, so he walked back up the street, where music could be heard coming from the doors and open windows of the saloons. The best he could find was a chili parlor and flat beer, and he managed to spill both on his uniform before the evening was over. When he returned to the hotel, a man in a fine suit and oiled hair parted in the middle of his head awaited him in the lobby. It was hot in there, and Sam noted that sweat and hair oil rolled down the sides of his head. "Sam Cook?" he queried. Sam nodded and smiled. "I am Mr. Darnell Baxter of the Chamber of Commerce, and I have come to give you instructions for tomorrow." He went on to tell Sam where to go, where to wait, what car to ride in, and how to wave. He wanted him to wave with his injured hand, since the public would not know him otherwise.

The next morning Sam waited at his assigned spot. Some women from the Daughters of the Confederacy, all wearing bright sashes, surrounded him and began bandaging his hand. "My hand is fine, ma'am." he said, but she told him that people would like it better if the wound looked a little fresher. She dabbed a little red paint on it to make it look like the wound had leaked a little. She also worked on a few chili spots on his tunic. Sam and the Daughters boarded a large convertible touring car, and he was placed with his butt on the trunk and his feet on the seat, so he rode above the rest. A smiley lady named Bess taught him how to wave to parade crowds. He practiced: elbow, elbow, wrist-wrist-wrist, as she had instructed. The big touring car pulled into the parade behind an elephant someone had wrangled from a traveling circus. A man led him, and both were decked out in red silky material with gold pendants and tassels. The car crept along. Sam waved and watched the twitching, defecating rear end of the elephant for more than an hour. When the parade was finally over, he was dropped off at the hotel where Lt. Murphy awaited him. He was given a train ticket and instructed to return to the station at eight the next morning for his return to Fort Bliss where he would be honorably discharged, given his war wounds and uselessness to the Army.

It was hardly past noon, and he did not know what to do with the rest of the day. Murphy had returned to the company of his girlfriend. It was hot, and he had not had breakfast, so he decided to find some shade and food. Sam

119

wanted to find the tamale stand he and Ed had eaten at before going to El Paso, but it had become a beer stand. He walked away, but then decided to get drunk, there being nothing better to do. The man at the little stand sold bottled beer, which Sam had not sampled before. He kept it on ice as well, and it was the best beer he had ever tasted. The proprietor recognized him from the parade and insisted that all of his beer was free. Soon a crowd gathered and Sam told the tale of his capture and torture so many times that he began to believe it himself. He had not had such celebrity since his first day at the Fairy school. His incomplete hand had become his lucky hand, again.

Sam spent the rest of the afternoon in a little café near the Stockyards nursing a headache and drinking coffee. After most of a pot of coffee and half a peach pie, he felt well enough to go back to the pens one more time. He thought of Ed, and the kindnesses he had shown him. He decided he would find him in Waco as soon as he had been discharged. The pens had plenty of cattle, but more mules and donkeys than he had ever seen in one place. Sam asked a boy cleaning pens why there were so many. "The war in Europe," he said. "Them French are buying them up for the war or for eatin', or maybe both." Sam had been only slightly aware of the new hostilities, and had thought little about them. If they needed that many mules, he thought, it must be a bad one coming.

Sam returned to his room well after dark. He smelled Kate's sweet smell before he saw her form, sitting in the shadow of the corner. She smelled like plums. She stood and embraced him. She had come on the same train as Sam, but had waited until his obligations were over to find him. She told him that the Red Cross was sending her to England, to help with the war wounded there.

She had come to say goodbye. She cried softly. Sam held her. "I don't know what to do, Sam." There were tears in her voice. "I love you and I want to stay here."

Sam was dumbstruck. After a long time, he whispered, "Stay with me! Just run away, Kate. That's all. I'll take care of you." Sam's nose started to run.

She wiped his nose with her handkerchief, and said, "I love you, Sam, but I have to go."

In the morning, a little stream of dusty sunlight came through the curtains. It was early. Sam woke. Her face was inches from his. She smiled. Sam and Kate smiled across the pillow like they were proud of their teeth. Her eyes held everything good; held everything in the world that was worth wanting. He embraced her, and felt the silk of her skin against his body. They made love, and then she was gone. He watched her through the pale lace curtains. She had a small suitcase and a little straw hat. She got smaller as she moved down the street. She came to a corner. She looked back once, but did not see him. She turned the corner and disappeared from sight. Sam wept so, he nearly missed his train.

CHAPTER 7

Sam returned to Fort Bliss and was discharged with little ceremony. After some searching, he found Ed at a hospital in Waco, which had been converted to treat the few casualties sustained on the border. He was in a long room with many windows and rows of beds, mostly unoccupied and neatly made. It was quiet except for the buzzing of flies on the window screens and the whoosh of big ceiling fans. The air was hot and still and it smelled of disinfectant. Ed's cot was in a corner where the light did not reach. He sat at the edge of his bed in a night gown staring at the floor. A mask covered one side of his face.

"Ed?" Sam called softly. Ed looked at Sam coming down the aisle of beds. A grin peeked out from the edge of a mask which covered half his face.

"You son-of-a-bitch!" he laughed. "I thought they had paraded you all the way to Washington D.C. and throwed you in the Potomac!" he howled.

Sam grinned and said "No they just painted my hand and made me watch a elephant take a shit!"

Ed had had four surgeries on his face, but they could not save his eye. He showed little sorrow for his loss, and told Sam that he thought he had done worse to some Mexicans. Sam agreed that there had been many Mexican casualties in the street. Someone had laid them out in rows, he told Ed, but he wondered if anybody had come to take them home. Sam told Ed about his kidnap, and the courtesy with which he was treated, and the music and Mexican cigarettes.

Ed howled with laughter, "That was mary-jee-wanna, Sam!" He thought that was the funniest thing he had ever heard, especially about the old man who had farted and started Sam's laughing fit. Ed was not surprised that the Army had made the best they could of the story, but seemed a little let down that they had not similarly honored him.

"Well, I didn't feel honored, Ed. It was a lie, but it wasn't my lie." Sam said. Later, a nurse came into the ward and told Sam it was time to leave. He assured Ed that he would return in the morning.

Sam found a job sweeping floors in a boarding house near the hospital. It was filled with pretty girls, and they let him sleep on a cot in a lean-to on the back of the house. Though he was inexperienced, it did not take him long to realize that it was a bordello. They thought Sam was an innocent country boy, and teased and doted on him. He gave such evidence of green-ness by avoiding looking at the provocatively dressed girls when he came down stairs, and digging the toe of his shoe into the rug when they spoke to him. They soon learned of his service and celebrity, and treated him with more deference than he deserved, he thought. He did not tell them the true story, since the lie seemed to benefit his situation there. Ed was released from the hospital, and Sam arranged for another cot in the lean-to. Ed swept floors and Sam tended to the lawn and gardening. They shared the wages. Since they were fed and housed along with the other employees, Sam saw any remuneration as sheer profit. It allowed the two to get some new clothes and some treats such as candy and occasionally alcohol, of which Ed increasingly imbibed.

One of the girls was sympathetic to Ed's disfigurement, and began selling him time for a fraction of the usual fee. Ed was broke for much of the time he and Sam lived under that arrangement, which came to an end a few months after they had settled there. This and a few other "bawdy houses" had been tolerated by the citizens of Waco for several decades, but the onset of the war and the influx of soldiers made the city fathers squeamish about the poor influence the girls might have on the military. The view seemed funny to Sam: that boys being trained to kill other boys might be sullied by consorting with whores. In any case, it was time for Sam and Ed to move on, and neither wanted to stay around Waco.

They decided to walk up the Brazos River for a way, since they had some money and wanted entertainment. They also wanted an opportunity to develop a plan for their future support. Neither wanted to return to the stockyards, and thought they might be businessmen — storekeepers, perhaps. Sam bought a single-shot .22 rifle, and believed they could live on squirrels and fish and pecans until they found something better. They both wanted to go north anyway, and the thought of returning to Hamilton, though risky, had crossed Sam's mind more than once. No one was left there that he particularly wanted to see, and several were there who might want to harm him if his identity were known. But all the same, it was what he thought of as home. They walked to a river bridge and spent the night under it. The weather was already showing signs of fall and turning colder. They were not well supplied for winter and wanted to make it to their journey's end and form a new plan before winter came in earnest.

The Brazos was red and muddy, and its banks crumbled as they walked out of town. There were no trees on either side of the river, the land having been cropped to the edge of each bank. The day was slate gray; the soil was bare and just as muddy red as the river. A misty cold wind blew out of the north. "Falling down in the mud ain't the adventure I had in mind, Sam, I coulda got drunk and done that in Waco." grumbled Ed, who had just had his boot sucked off by river bank ooze. Sam said that he thought the trees would begin to hold the bank together after they had gotten further north, and that they would find forests like he had seen on the Leon. The land did not improve, however, but became more gullied, more ruined the further they travelled. It wasn't until the third day that they came upon a little fringe of forest along the river. The day was turning rainy, and they decided to camp for a day or two to try to find some food. The little forest had no pecan trees, but plenty of squirrels. After half a box of bullets, Sam brought down three squirrels. They found a little spit of land in the river, which was an island when the water was higher. Black willow and bloodweed covered the acre or so and it was hard to find a spot clear enough to settle. After some searching, they found an opening near the center of the island, where it was gravelly and the plants sparse. The thickets around them held off the wind and blowing rain. They built a fire out of driftwood and bent a few willow saplings over to make a shelter. The squirrels were cooked and found greasy, and Ed said they were old squirrels. "It'll make a turd, though." he grunted. At this hungry point in the journey it was sufficient praise.

A few more squirrels were taken and their charred remains were wrapped up in leaves for the trip. They continued up river. The little gallery forest continued, screening miles of plowed and muddy cotton field. Eventually, the land became hilly and for the first time they saw ash and pecan trees and scattered oaks. They loaded up their sacks with pecans after they had eaten all they could hold. The hills showed bare limestone in spots. Scrawny red oaks and little ash trees stood out red and gold on the hillsides in the gloom of the rainy skies. Ed had his army compass, which he checked with some regularity. "Sam, we keep walkin' half a day north and then half a day, south." He sounded pained. "There are so many bends and loops in this river, we are gettin' nowhere!" Sam said that he wanted to go north and west. He was thinking about going to Hamilton County. All that suited Ed who was relieved they had a destination. They agreed to take the next sizable creek to the left, and hope that its channel ran northwest, so they could follow it upstream.

The sky was clear in the morning. The rocky bluffs around them caught the light a long time before it warmed the river valley. They doused their fire and climbed a bluff to get some warmth and have a look around. The valley was dark. Patches of fog clung to the terraces above it, but the high land beyond glowed in strong gold light. "This looks like a better day to me," grinned Sam. They ate the bit of greasy squirrel and some pecans and began the walk upstream. The day was still and warm, and their ears buzzed with the silence when they stopped to listen, though Ed was not much for silence, and was uncomfortable if the conversation lagged. His mask had gotten moldy on the inside, and caused his skin to itch. He rinsed the mask in the muddy water, and stuffed it with some cotton, which he had gleaned earlier from the fields. Sam tried not to look, but saw that the right side of his face looked like melted candle wax.

Late in the day, they came upon the confluence of the Brazos and a sizeable creek, which appeared to run generally southeast, and which came clean and clear out of the limestone country to the west. Where the waters of the muddy river and the clear creek came together, there was a stream of clear water which made up almost half of the river channel. Sam stood on a rocky ledge and, shading his eyes, could see fish congregating where the waters came together. He put a little greasy squirrel on a fish hook and cast a line. Ed was upstream flipping rocks and catching crawdads. It wasn't long before Sam had caught four bream and a little catfish. He put the mess into a pot along with the crawdads Ed had caught and boiled them until all had turned to mush. Full for the first time in several days, they lounged the afternoon away, and slept through the night.

The country along the stream was rocky. Bluffs enclosed the creek, which became narrower the further they traveled. By the third day, the creek was little more than a trickle with a few potholes holding deeper water. The range around the creek was hard used, and the water in the potholes was scummy. They were camped at the edge of the stream when an old man on horseback splashed up the creek. He had gray whiskers with tobacco stains in them and a large belly, against which he holstered a large pistol. "Goldang, if you boys don't look like you run from the circus." he sneered. "What tore y'all up so?" Ed explained that they were veterans from the late skirmish with Pancho Villa. The old man ruminated and spit tobacco juice into the wind, the effect being that that which did not blow back on his shirt dribbled through his dirty whiskers. Is that so?" He dismounted, walked over to the camp and squinted at Ed's mask and then at Sam's hand. "Well, since you are all war heroes, I guess I won't run ya off, this bein' my place and all. But if you are gonna stay here, you'll have to work for your lodgin'. I judge that you've not et well in some time, so I will throw in some beans as well." Both were amenable to the idea. "I had about two hundred head of Merino sheep and the bloody scours took all of em but twenty. They's pretty much fly blowed by now, but that wool is still worth pullin'. Will be easier now that they rotten."

Most of the sheep were in or near the sheep shed and pens. The stench was terrible, but both Sam and Ed had encountered its equal or worse at the stock yards. The wool came off the carcasses easily enough, though frequently the hide came with it exposing writhing maggots below. Ed became accustomed to interrupting his monologue long enough to turn aside and retch. The long day ended with beans and corn bread, a luxury they had not had in a long time. The next day, they helped the man drag the carcasses to a pile, where he would burn them.

Sam asked "If you were gonna make Hamilton from here, how would you go?"

The man scratched his belly and spit, away from the wind this time. "This creek crosses the Waco road up north of here somewhere. But to go by field lanes to the road is gonna make ya run south first. I suppose the Creek is probably the most direct way."

The boys washed the stench of sheep carcass out of their clothes at the man's windmill. They packed their few belongings along with some biscuits the man had given them, said farewell and returned to the creek. The banks of the creek became brushy as soon as they left the boundary fence of the sheep farm. Dogwoods, greenbriers, and plums were so thick the boys walked the center of the channel, and jumped the pools. The bottom was hard limestone and fairly dry. The walking was easy. Once a buck, an unusual sight, flushed as they rounded a bend. Sam tried to shoot it with the little .22, but by the time he chambered a shell, the buck was nothing but the sound of brush crashing in the distance. They camped cold on the creek and ate their biscuits. The little bit of squirrel started to smell, so they did with what they had. The next day, they heard the Waco road before they saw it. Every time a wagon or automobile crossed it, they could hear the pop and groan of the bridge suspension. They clambered up to the road and were able to hail a famer taking a load of hogs all the way to Hamilton.

CHAPTER 8

Within a few days, they had landed some odd jobs, including helping a peddler. The old man, named Harris, had a cart, laden with little things like needles, thread, flyswatters, and kitchen utensils. He had started with a hand cart, which he trundled up and down the steep hills around Pecan Creek, which ran through the middle of town. He had since acquired a mule to pull a new cart, but found it a boon to get the hand cart back into service. Sam and Ed were, in his estimate, young and sprangly enough to do just that. They rang the bell on the little cart and sometimes knocked on doors. Sam was assigned the job of pitching the sale, because Ed was, with his face hidden behind the half mask, a little frightening. Harris decided to mount a sign on the cart, announcing that the wares were being sold by war heroes. This improved business somewhat, and explained their disfigurement, though the customers, mainly women and girls, still kept their distance from Ed. It hurt his feelings a bit, since this was his first experiences with the fairer sex since his injury which was not a commercial transaction. Sam assured him that the right woman would come along. Ed was not so sure.

Harris put them up in a small house next to the creek. It had been his original home, but prosperity had moved him to a better part of the town. Pecan Creek was notorious for flooding, and the frame house was warped and moldy as a result of having spent so much time under water. It had a small cook stove, which, given the condition of the rest of the house, drew surprisingly well. Sam was impressed by it and was inspired to cook, though he had had little instruction other than the times he had tried to help Mutt in the kitchen, or had watched her while she prepared the best food he had eaten. Sam managed to fry bacon and heat cans of stewed tomatoes and beans. Though he tried several times to bake white bread, his efforts were disasters. Having been raised on corn bread and little else, white bread held an association with good times and hopes for better times to come. He decided it would be one luxury he would spend his meager wages on.

A German family lived on the south side of town, and a woman there baked bread for sale. Her beautiful loaves were sometimes sold from the peddler's cart, but Sam knew he could get it cheaper if he bought it directly. On the way, he intended to mail a week's worth of letters to Kate, in care of the Red Cross in England. He missed her sorely, and had, within days of establishing a residence, sent her a letter with his mailing address.

It was a bright, dry November day, warm with a little breeze blowing in from the southwest. Sam felt at home for the first time since he had lived with Gus and Mutt in Fairy. He walked south on Rice, the main street, and found the house selling bread by following his nose. The place was small and tidy, and small tidy children played in the yard. He bought two loaves. The crusts were hard, shiny and pale gold, and he broke one and had eaten half the loaf by the time he neared the courthouse. A tall man with a droopy mustache watched him from the shadow of a doorway. He eventually caught up with Sam.

"What's your name, son?" Sam turned to him, his mouth so full of bread he could not answer quickly.

"Sam Cook, sir." he said with half a mouthful. Sheriff Jenson narrowed his eyes and studied Sam's face for a moment.

The Sheriff said, "You look familiar, and your right hand looks mighty familiar." He asked Sam to accompany him to the courthouse, where he seated him in a hard chair in front of his desk. Jenson did not speak, but rifled through the drawers of his desk until he found an old wanted poster describing Sam. He looked at Sam, then smiled and rubbed his face with his hands. "You *are* Sam Wood", he said, but not threateningly. "I also know who Sam Cook is. I was in Fort Worth when he was celebrated as the man who did not give up his nation's secrets under torture." Sam felt the bread lodge somewhere between his stomach and his windpipe. He gripped the arms of his chair.

The Sheriff told Sam that he needed to hold him till he got it all sorted out. Sam was handcuffed and led to a little building near the courthouse. His cell was on the second floor. It was not more than six feet to a side. The bars were flat and woven into a mesh that did not allow much light or air to penetrate. Though he was filled with dread, he mostly mourned the loss of his loaf and a half of white bread. The jailer had taken his shoes, his money and his bread. The Sheriff did not return for the remainder of the day, and most of the next. The food, however, was better than he had recently eaten, though corn bread was served with each meal.

On the afternoon of the second day, Sam was taken from his cell and led, without handcuffs, back to the courthouse. The Sheriff, county judge, and the mayor were sitting in the

Sheriff's office. The mayor and judge nodded to Sam as they were introduced. They did not smile. The Sheriff did most of the talking. "Sam, what are you doing in Hamilton?" Sam tried to explain about home, and family, but got tongue-tied. He did aver that he had never stolen cattle nor murdered anyone. "I know that, Sam. They found Carpenter's turkeys on Bilch's place a week after you went to Gatesville, and Bilch found all of his cattle. From what I can tell, Charlie Buck probably saved you from being murdered. We never did find him, though. We had heard you were killed in a storm at the Boy's School and figured that was the end of it. In any case, the judge and mayor and I agree there is no good to be had prosecuting a war hero and having to argue the story of your torture with the army." Sam wondered why they had not gotten him out of Gatesville when they knew the truth, but there was nothing to be done for it now. "Ruder Bilch is dead." said Jenson. "Shot by one of his hands last year, so you won't have to avoid him. Only a handful of cowhands are left around from that time, but you would do well to lay low. I would suggest, but won't insist that you move on." The Sheriff opened the door for Sam, and he found his way down the dark courthouse corridor to the bright light outside.

Sam hurried to find Ed, who would be pushing the cart by himself. He had already missed a half day's work. He found Ed at the top of the hill west of the square. He was sitting by the cart, trying to catch his breath. Sam sat beside him, and said "Ed, I got something to tell you." Sam laid out the story of his life up to the point that he and Ed had met in the stockyard. Ed stared a long moment at Sam when he was finished, then punched him in the arm and smiled.

"Think I'm gonna call you Sam Cookwood since your bread is about like a chunk a wood." He got up. "Shit, I didn't know I was goin' about with a fugitive." he giggled. They pushed the cart down the street. There were four loaves of the German lady's bread on the cart. Sam bought them all.

CHAPTER 9

On Saturday, the square was bustling. Sam and Ed pushed the cart into the throng and almost sold the entire inventory before noon. Many people from the surrounding farms and ranches came to Hamilton on Saturdays to shop and to sell. On this Saturday, the square was even more crowded as the darling of the Women's Christian Temperance Movement, and candidate for United States Senator, Morris Stevens was to give a speech. The usual Saturday traffic along with those who came to attend the speech bloated the usual population. Therefore, more people would be in earshot of the candidate's "clarion call, and amplification, & etc." whether they cared to hear it or not. By noon the square thronged with wagons and carriages and not a few automobiles. The dais had been assembled at the front steps of the courthouse. Some of the county employees occupied their offices with family in order to hang out of the windows for the best views. Mischievous children dropped scraps of paper confetti as well as spit soaked wads down on the hatted assembly below. A few hands from surrounding ranches were released for their monthly trip to town. This necessary "airing out" of mostly young men and boys included barbering, a bath and expunging of the various bad habits and tendencies which were kept tamped down under the gaze of their bosses. By afternoon, the cowboys had bathed and been shaved, and most had settled into their primary occupation for the remainder of the day: drinking. There were several saloons to choose from. The cowboys gathered in front of the Basement saloon, bottles and glasses in hand, to ogle the proceedings. They were in turn ogled by several members of the WCTM who peered down their noses at such an acute angle that one might have thought they depended on gravity to keep their eyeballs in their sockets.

The honorable Stevens mounted the podium just as a shoving match erupted over by the saloon. It was not aggressive, but emanated from playful joshing over one boy's embarrassment at having been caught mooning over one of the ladies on the stand. They were not all old. Mr. Stevens paused and looked on disdainfully at the crowd of cowboys. A Deputy Sheriff rose slowly and ambled over to the saloon, hoping his presence there would keep rowdiness to a low simmer. Ed and Sam moved to the south side of the square and climbed a tree to get a better view. Mr. Stevens began his speech:

> "Gentlemen and ladies of Hamilton County: It is my honor to be here with you today, and my sorrow that the great hall of justice upon whose steps I stand are ringed by no less than six saloons. I have traveled across the great state of Texas delivering the message of temperance, and decrying the legal debauchery offered in each of these dens of iniquity. It is no large task for me to tell you the reasons these "whitewashed sepulchers" should be closed down and driven from our midst. But I have found, just as did our Lord and savior, that edification of the many must come from the parable. I want to tell you now, of a true story. One that took place in Abilene, but could just as well have been Hamilton, or Stephenville, or Dallas.
>
> A man, who had led a sober and productive life, killed his only daughter, a tow-headed beauty of twelve. Let us call her Betty. Blue eyes, and, according to those

who knew and loved her, the sweetest disposition of any child in that fair city. The father, let us call him "Gus", ran a prosperous cotton farm, had a fine house and many hands to tend to both. But then his fortunes began to turn. He had made some poor investments. The arrival of the rail spur to his cotton farm was delayed. Because of this he had cotton in the field which was not worth picking. The many loans he had taken to make his house and home prosperous were coming due. The wolf, gentlemen and ladies, was at the door. This was a black time for Gus. His secrets he shared not with family, friends, his pastor —oh yes, he was a God fearing and church going man. Instead he turned to... a saloon; to a bottle and a bar tender. *Oh, the offense.* These gates of hell sanctioned by judge, by commissioner, by voters like you were the undoing of this man. Night after night, Gus numbed his very soul with whiskey, while he became a stranger to his wife and his daughter and his *God*! So distraught was the poor girl that she walked to the saloon! In the middle of the night! To plead for her father's return to the safety and sanctity of home! Of church! One can only imagine the trepidation with which this child pushed open those hated swinging doors to a dimly lit, smoke filled hell. The foul smell of tobacco, of alcohol, of dirty stinking souls in peril of utter and eternal damnation! She found her father at the back of the saloon. His head lay unconscious on the table amidst a litter of playing cards, empty glasses and an empty whisky bottle. She gently shook his shoulder. "Oh Daddy." she said. "Please come home with me!" she cried. She wept such piteous tears, that even the addled mind and stone heart of a drunkard could not help but to be moved. "Oh my dearest, sweetest daughter. I will come with you. I will try, with God's help, to be a better man." She took his arm as he unsteadily made his way to the street, where his buggy was tied. With her help, he was seated and took the reins. No amount of this child's love, nor the greatness of his regrets could have improved his judgment at that moment. For before his precious daughter could lift herself into the carriage, he slapped reins across the back of the horse, which bolted, and young Betty was crushed beneath the wheels of the carriage, one wheel collapsing her head like a ripe melon!"

A gasp passed through the attending crowd and a flurry of fanning of overheated and flushed faces swept through the WCTM ladies on the dais. One vomited, then fainted and was attended to by the deputy, who had returned from his visit with the rowdies. Of these, two of the cowboys wept openly, though they continued to swig their bottles.

Mr. Stevens's speech continued for another hour in more or less the same vein. His primary strategy appeared to be condemnation of those who came to hear him. It seemed to Sam that this would be an ineffective way to campaign. However, by the end of his speech he made it clear that absolution could only be guaranteed by seeing to it that he made it to Washington, D.C., a far greater den of iniquity than Hamilton. "Dang." Ed murmured. "Looks like if they have their way, alcohol is gonna get scarce. I'm gonna have to start makin' my own again."

CHAPTER 10

Mr. Harris was so pleased with the income Ed and Sam brought in that he turned the peddling over to them and opened a store on the square. Ed continued with the push cart in town, and Sam worked the surrounding country with the mule. With the additional income they were able to improve Mr. Harris's house. Of particular joy to Sam was the shoring up of the porch which wrapped around the front of the house and the side facing the creek. Sam had taken to the happiness of sitting on Mabel's porch as a child, and especially enjoyed watching the creek bottoms darken as the sun went down. Sam's cooking improved. Mrs. Harris gave Sam a sourdough starter which she said she had gotten from her mother, many years before. The little loaves of white bread Sam made were beautiful, hard crusted, yeasty and tinged with oak wood smoke. He baked weekly, and Ed put on fifteen pounds. "Alright, Cookwood, I guess I can call you Cookgood, now." said Ed with his mouthful of Sam's bread. Sam grinned at him and bounced a little loaf off the top of Ed's head.

Business fell off during the winter. Most of the roads in Hamilton and all of them in the country were mud. There were still sales to be made, but getting to the buyer was becoming almost impossible. Mr. Harris allowed the boys to stay there on Pecan Creek. In exchange, they painted the rooms with the paint that did not sell from the carts. They ate with the Harris's on Wednesday nights, and it was that meal which kept up their morale.

Following dinner on a cold and wet night, Mr. Harris sipped his coffee and pondered. The previous summer, he had acquired a property along the river. The place had a little cabin and forty acres. He had gotten it at the county auction for taxes owed. He offered it to them, and suggested they could pay it off over several years. The one stipulation was that it be improved somehow. "The person who lived there was a poor housekeeper. The fields are grown up in locust trees, and there is no privy." he grimaced. Harris was fastidious in his own habits and was dismayed when he stumbled across those who weren't. When the weather and roads dried up some, they decided to see the property. They borrowed a mule, mounted tandem, and followed a map north and east from town to the river. A dim road took them through a cedar brake which ended at the edge of a bluff overlooking the river bottom. A dingy little cabin sat back in the trees. Sam checked the mule, dumbstruck. "That's Charlie Buck's cabin." he said, almost whispering.

They rode the mule down the bluff and up to the door of the cabin. The cabin leaned slightly toward the river. It had been sided with pine planks, but in spots the old post oak logs showed through. It had three windows. One still had a glass pane or two. Sam opened the door and was over-whelmed by the smell of skunk. They opened the back door to air it out a bit.

Sam said, "Skunks will move in like that in the winter. He'll be gone soon enough."

Ed said without much of his usual humor, "Livin' on the creek and pushing a cart suits me just fine. At least we don't have to smell skunk when we come in the door." They decided to look around the acreage. It was, as Mr. Harris said, grown up in locust trees, but it was clear that it had been farmed. The trees were young, and the rocks had been moved from the field and stacked in neat fences along its edge. Sam gathered up some soil and smelled it. "Dang, it almost smells like my sourdough, it's so good." He held it out for Ed to whiff, and he had to agree that it did smell fertile. Between the two of them, they decided they had about one-half of a farmer's knowledge, though. At the back of the land, the woods were thick. Young hackberry trees screened the deeper forest nearer the river, where the canopy of red and bur oak and elms stood high above an open floor. Ed noticed some junk piled near a little hillock. Their investigation revealed the remnants of Charlie's old still. Most of it seemed to be there, and reasonably intact. Ed picked up a copper tube and grinned. "I got me an idea. I think I want to buy this place."

They agreed to continue working for Mr. Harris during the week and working the field and on the cabin in their spare time — of which there was little. When summer finally came and the roads were open again, they plied their wares. Five and one-half days a week, they worked in Hamilton and slept in the house on the creek. On Saturday afternoon, they rented a mule and headed for the river. They planned to resurrect the overgrown field. They cut thorny honey locusts to the ground with borrowed tools and poured coal oil on the stumps to make them rot. The work was hard and sweat poured into Sam's eyes, but there was an atmosphere of holiday, though by Sunday night their arms bled and they had holes in their clothes from the thorns. He and Ed would plant corn here, and part would go to making liquor (an art which Ed claimed to know) and part would be sold for feed. By the middle of summer, they had the field cleared, but not plowed. They did not have a team or a plow and would have to hire it done. Ed found a neighbor a few miles upriver; a retired farmer, who still kept a team of mules and had a plow he called a "ripper." Its chisel teeth were sufficient to pull up the roots of little trees. Once it was "ripped" he said, he could bring a mule and a moldboard plow and then a harrow. His was their only offer of help, though he wanted fifty dollars. The farmer, a man named Winkler, carried a flask in his back pocket. He swigged from it to punctuate his sentences, or when the conversation got lively or when it lagged. Ed had an idea. He would provide Winkler corn liquor of the finest quality for one year in payment. By the time the deal was made, the payment agreed to was five dollars and one year's supply.

In late summer, Winkler returned. It took four trips between his place and theirs to move the equipment and team. He brought a nephew with him. He was a mean-eyed little man who wore greased hair and a sneer that made him look like he was always on the verge of spitting. He wore his cap cocked at an angle, which Sam thought was a sure sign of belligerence. When he saw Ed's mask, he hooted and asked, "You escaped from the circus or something?" Ed explained the battle in New Mexico and the wound he received. The sneery little man, whose name was Puddy Baker, replied, "That little scuffle ain't nothing compared to what's goin' on over there", he poked his thumb in the direction he thought "over there" might be, though he wasn't sure, so he changed his mind and poked it in another direction. He announced when he got "over there" the Germans wouldn't last long. Ed proceeded to ignore him, which was not to Puddy's liking.

Sam watched Puddy follow Ed around the field and interrupt him when he spoke to Winkler, who seemed only vaguely aware of the nuisance he had brought with him. Winkler told Puddy to hitch the team to the ripper and commented to Ed, grinning, "What he lacks in size, he shore makes up for in piss and vinegar, don't he?" Sam heard the comment and wondered if the man was proud of him or was being apologetic.

The field was "ripped" and the little locust roots and stumps came up without much fuss. Winkler ran the team and the implement with such finesse, that it didn't matter that he swigged from a bottle of brown liquor and was otherwise staggering drunk. Puddy, Sam and Ed piled the stumps to burn later. The ripping took all day, and by sunset, the team had been watered and fed, and Puddy and Winkler had built a campfire near the house. They had brought sardines and canned meat and whiskey with them. Sam gave them a loaf of bread. Since they were camped by the house, and the house was too hot to sleep in anyway, Sam and Ed pulled pallets to the fire and made preparations to sleep there. After a bit of potted meat and some whiskey, Puddy was sufficiently energetic to resume bullying Ed. He reached for Ed's face saying

"Lemme see what's under that dang thing." Ed slapped his hand down. "Nobody touches me but what I ask for it." Puddy hissed, his eyes narrowed.

"Looks to me like you asked for it." Winkler chuckled. Puddy stood and beckoned to Ed.

"You come up here and I'll show you what a man is." He threw his cap in the dust. He windmilled his fists and

145

hollered, "C'mon, masky-face! Let's see what you got." Ed rose and threw a half-hearted punch at Puddy. Puddy hopped away from the punch and laughed like a lunatic. He tried to kick Ed in the knee, but Ed caught his boot heel and almost flipped him into the fire. He pinned Puddy to the ground and tore the mask off. He pressed his ruined face into Puddy's and whispered, "Is this what you wanna see?" He pressed closer, "This better? Can ya see it now?" He pressed his gullied, sweaty cheek into Puddy's eye socket. Puddy screamed and gagged, and flailed his legs until Ed let him up.

"This ain't the end of it." Puddy whimpered. He packed his gear and stalked out beyond the firelight. Winkler snickered until Puddy was beyond earshot, and then had a good belly laugh.

"Galldern, son." he choked on his laughter. "Put that thing back on or I'll be havin' nightmares."

Sam was speechless. He never saw a bully so cowed, nor seen Ed so worked up. Ed's injury was no laughing matter, and it made him a little sorry that they had hired Winkler and Puddy. Ed sat next to Sam and slapped him on the knee. "Guess I settled him." he grinned.

Winkler said, "Oh, no, Puddy ain't one to give up a grudge too quick. You better watch your back for a while." The work proceeded without a flaw the next day, and by sunset, the field was plowed, ripped and harrowed. The smell of fresh turned chocolate earth was intoxicating. That it had lain fallow since long before Charlie's death had sweetened it. Charlie had told Sam that land had a heart. You could graze, and cut and plow and grow only to a certain point.

Beyond that, the land's heart broke. He said much of the land he knew was heartbroken, and would never come back. Sam could tell from the smell of this sweet ground that its heart was whole.

Winkler spent another night and drank a prodigious amount of whiskey. He told stories about the Spanish war, and the girls he had known, and how his paw had fought the Comanches and the Mexicans. Nevertheless, he was up before Sam or Ed in the morning, singing and making coffee on the campfire. Since Puddy never returned, Sam helped him make the four trips necessary to get his implements and team back to his farm. Winkler suggested that they scatter oats on the field to keep it covered over winter. They would hand - sow the corn in the spring.

CHAPTER 11

Spring of 1918 was wet and muddy. There was little work to do for Mr. Harris as the roads had stayed impassable for months. Sam and Ed shared the wages from the push cart, and eventually agreed that Ed would take residence on the farm, and repair the house, plant corn and build the still. Sam would push the cart alone. Letters from Kate had been few over the winter, but had begun to increase in the spring. The letters were short, but told of the horror of the wounded, who came into the London hospital without ceasing. Some boys were gassed and could not talk or even breathe; many were dismembered and disfigured. Many were dying of an influenza which no one had ever seen. They simply became sick and were dead within a few days. She wrote that she believed the war would end soon, since the United States had joined the effort. When it did, she dreamed of returning to Sam. He had written her of his and Ed's partnership, though he did not mention bootlegging. He was sure she would disapprove.

Wages were short, as was food. Sam had sufficient flour to make bread, but had turned to the woods along the river for other provender. Deer were scarce, but varmints such as raccoons and possums were abundant, as were squirrels and fish. By late spring, dewberries and pokeweed were so abundant and appeared on the table so frequently that the laxative effect gave them both diarrhea. On his days off, Sam ranged farther into the river bottom and followed the channel so far north that the river forest began to thin out. Beyond the channel few trees grew, and the grass was thin. Early one morning, he heard strange sounds coming from beyond the river bank. The sound was like someone blowing into the neck of a bottle. He crept up the side of the channel and peered over. A few hundred feet away were gathered short round birds. Two or three occupied the center of a group of admirers. They strutted with tails fanned and inflated funny little balloons on their cheeks. Each time the balloons popped up the funny sound was emitted. Sam had heard of prairie chickens, but had never seen one. It was reported that they were highly edible. Though a shotgun would be preferred, Sam decided to try his .22. The sharp crack scattered the birds, which were slow getting off the ground and did not fly far. A small brown body lay near the dancing circle. Sam followed the little flock until he had four hens, enough to make a meal. He returned to the house an hour or two before sunset, where he found Ed waiting for him. He was grinning from ear to ear.

"Guess who I saw in town?" he said, looking at Sam from under his eyebrow and still grinning. Sam was puzzled.

"Go on, Ed! Who'd ya see?"

Ed handed Sam a scarf. "She said to give ya this." Sam's eyes filled and he sat down.

"Kate? Kate's here?"

Ed doubled up in laughter and slapped his knee. "Well I guess old Ed better be findin' another place, I reckon." Sam did not know what to say. He handed the prairie chickens to Ed and found the mule hobbled and grazing not too far from the house.

"I'll see you next weekend, Ed!!" he hollered as he trotted the mule west to town.

Kate had been relieved of duty at the end of April, and had made travel arrangements to cross the Atlantic home. Though she mailed a letter to Sam announcing her intentions, she felt certain that she would get home days ahead of her letter. Her time in London had taken much from her. She hoped the trip would help her lose some of the grief she had stored for many months, but its residue stayed with her. Nightmares and uncontrollable eruptions of searing grief were regular. She had taken the train to Hamilton without letting her Illinois family know she was back. She had found a room in a boarding house near the square. She had seen Ed in town on Saturday morning and had asked him to send word to Sam to meet her. She expected him at any time.

Sam found Kate seated on the porch of the boarding house. She had not seen him, and it gave him a chance to admire her before she composed herself. She wore a white dress, buttoned to the chin. Her black hair was cut short, and she looked out into the street without expression; her lips parted. She was lovely, but she did not look well or happy. Sam spent a few more moments in adoration, and then opened the little gate from the street. He stopped. He had imagined all of the things he would say to her; how he would open his heart to her; say things that would make her want to stay. He could only stare and grin. Kate rose from her seat and came to Sam. She met his eye and tried to smile. Instead she put her face in his shoulder and wept. "It was hard, Sam." she sobbed. "I have come back, but I don't think all of me made it home." Sam held her and softly spoke little nonsense words in her ear.

For several days, Kate followed Sam and his push cart. They talked between sales. Sam talked of the border and their time together, and the ridiculous parade, and his and Ed's walk up the Brazos. She talked about the poor soldiers and the nurses and doctors she had worked with. They were not all good, the doctors. A few, especially among the surgeons, cared more about their reputations and position than they did for their patients. Because most of the town was aware of her and why she was there, she did not visit Sam in the little house on Pecan Creek, nor did he visit her at the boarding house, which had strict rules about guests of the opposite gender. Instead, they met for walks along the creek, and when they were sufficiently hidden, kissed. Kate accompanied Sam to the river on his next trip. He described the event as a campout with a picnic, and he planned ways to make it as pleasant as possible, though he was worried the sorry state of the shack would disappoint her.

On the following Saturday, Sam rented a buggy and horse. It was early June, and a rain the night before had left a dazzling blue sky behind. The little road descended down the rocky river terraces. Sam stopped to show Kate the wildflowers which grew up between the rocks. Charlie had taught him the Comanche names for many of them, which he had forgotten, but he had also learned a few English names as well. He was proud that he could name them for Kate: the beardtongue, prairie clovers and one which made her laugh — the fringed puccoon. The air was heavy with their fragrance. He picked a bouquet of prairie phlox, the most perfumed. Kate was dressed in white, and carried a parasol. Color had returned to her cheeks and she looked happy. Sam could not take his eyes from her face, and he leaned in to kiss her, softly.

It was afternoon when they arrived at the cabin. Ed had collected more wildflowers and had filled buckets and empty bottles with them. He had found a vine with red berries which he had woven into a garland and hung above the doorway.

When the buggy rolled into the dooryard, he grinned so hard it looked like his jaw would break. "Y'all get down!" he hollered, and made a sweeping bow so low that his fingers dragged the ground. Sam laughed so hard he nearly fell out of the buggy. He came to Kate's side and helped her down.

"Ed's a kinda clown." said Sam, looking at the ground and scratching his ear.

Kate and Ed walked to the house together, and Ed told her about his surgeries and the difficult time he had being disfigured. He poured out his doubts that he would ever be loved. It irritated Sam, slightly, that Ed had such big feelings he had only referred to in passing with him. However, Ed brightened up and swung open the door to the cabin. Sam saw that the fireplace had been mortared, the stove blacked, the floor patched and even the missing panes of glass covered in wax paper.

"How do you like your nest?" he asked Kate. She blushed and turned to Sam.

"It's just fine, Ed, but I won't be staying long." Sam pretended that he had not heard her, and suggested they show Kate the fields and the river. They packed blankets and a box of food into the buggy and followed a dim trail into the river forest. A little breeze stirred the leaves of the canopy so that thousands of shafts of sunlight streaked to the forest floor. They spread their blankets in the dappled shade, and prepared to eat lunch. Ed had not had much to work with, but brought out some of Sam's bread, dewberries and the four prairie chickens, roasted over the resurrected fire place.

"Do you think these chickens have turned?" Sam sniffed one of the little carcasses.

"Hell, no!" protested Ed. "We always aged our fowl before cookin' em." He pulled a quart jar from the box and swirled the contents and grinned. "Besides, I got somethin' strong enough to disinfect our stomachs even if they have turned."

They ate their lunches and passed around the jar. The wind blew from the north, and the wooded bottoms held on to some of the coolness. Sam was surprised how much liquor Kate consumed. She was tipsy, but happy, though. Given the sadness he had seen in her, he was glad for it. After dozing on the blankets, they packed up the buggy and rode over to the cornfield. Young corn stood a foot high. The deep green leaves shined in the sun. Sam told Kate how the land was tilled, and the sweet smell of the soil. Ed started to explain the corn's use, but Sam interrupted before Ed could expand on the manufacture of sour mash. When they returned to the house it was late in the day, and Ed proposed that they build a campfire and finish the leftovers from lunch. Sam and Kate walked the edge of the woods to collect firewood.

"Sam, I have to go home to Illinois for a while," Kate said as she pulled some twigs from a bramble. "It has been a long time since I have seen my family, and my parents are getting old."

"Will you come back, Kate?" asked Sam. Since he had heard her comment about leaving, he had wanted to ask. "Of course, Sam. I just need some time."

The mood around the campfire was light hearted, and Ed sang "Dan Tucker" and danced a jig and patted juba. Kate had never seen such a performance and laughed so, she could hardly breathe. Sam was a little jealous that he was not as entertaining as Ed, but happy that Kate was so amused. They finished the liquor, and fixed pallets by the fire. Sam slept heavily until he heard the shuffle of Kate's footsteps. She was not on her pallet. He looked for her, and found her on her knees behind a low thicket at the edge of the yard. She was sick; had vomited. "Oh, Sam, I think that prairie chicken must have been bad." she croaked. Sam went to the house and got a wet rag and some water for her. He held her hair as she was sick again.

As Sam ministered to Kate, he heard the sound of hoof beats, and saw a half dozen men ride up to the fire in long white robes and hoods. "Get up, you cur!!!" hollered the one in front. They did not dismount. Ed rose and rubbed the sleep out of his good eye. "It is known that you drink, and make corn liquor and that you are a Godless heathen who don't attend church." The man pointed down at Ed. There were grunts of agreement from the others.

"Puddy Baker, I know that's you." said Ed. "You can take off that hood, and if you wanna fight me, get off the horse." A few of the others snickered.

"Let this be a warnin' to you, Ed Wright." He sounded peeved. "It will be far worse next time." The group wheeled their horses and rode into the field and trampled Ed's corn.

There was nothing Ed could do but watch. He sat by the fire, took off his mask and rubbed his scars.

Sam and Kate watched from the edge of the yard. "Who are they?" whispered Kate.

"I think it's Puddy Baker and some of his friends." Sam sighed. "Puddy don't like Ed."

In the morning, they assessed the damage to the corn field. Ed tried to prop a few stalks up, but it was a total loss. "Guess I will have to buy corn for a while." he grinned, though he looked pained.

Kate was distant when Sam took her back to town. He explained about the hired hands and the mean little man who Ed embarrassed. "Well, it sounds like Puddy is a coward," she said, "but it seems to me that you and Ed are living rough and have made some bad decisions, to draw in a bad sort like him." Sam agreed with her assessment, and tried to explain that his ambitions were greater than making moonshine on the Leon River. Kate said she disapproved of moonshining, though she didn't mind drinking it once in a while. Sam groped for words to make their parting momentous, but failed. He dropped her west of the square and she walked back to the boarding house to escape notice by onlookers. Within a few days, and after a few more words of parting, she was gone.

BOOK 3

CHAPTER 1

The end of the war came to Hamilton in the early morning hours of November 11, 1918. The square thronged with people who organized an anvil shoot. It was barely sunrise, and some still had on bedclothes. Many young men had been lost, but now the remnant could return home. Prohibition came a few years after the return of the veterans. Ed said it was unfortunate, because they all looked like they could have used a drink. Several wounded veterans had befriended Ed and the more so his still. One ex-soldier, a sallow boy named Dicky Ted, had a farm farther south on the river valley, and he had, after a year, and with the help of his friends completed a house. He was now in search of a bride to occupy it. The winter of 1922 was bitterly cold. Hard little snowflakes were born on the wind in front of the headlamps of Sam's Model-A Ford, which kept slipping in and out of the frozen ruts on the road to Ed's house. He was to pick him up and take him to Dicky Ted's for a Christmas party. Sam blew the claxon all the way down the drive to the house. Ed was waiting for him, and they began the trip down the valley to Dicky's. By the time they arrived, several boys lay face down on the porch with their heads hanging over the edge. They had had enough of Ed's liquor that they appreciated the convenience of a precipice to vomit from. When they got out of the car, Sam could hear scratchy fiddle music and stomping feet inside. The door was open despite the cold, and yellow light spilled across the porch and door yard. The furniture had been moved out, and twenty or more young men and women danced to the music. Sam accepted a drink from a quart jar, and leaned against the wall. A woman leaned against Sam and coyly pointed out a bed bug crawling up the wall next to him. She was drunk enough that she thought Sam would understand the allusion to bed as an invitation. Sam was not drunk enough to comprehend, though she made the requisite bedroom eyes at him. After a few minutes of silence from Sam, she moved on and leaned on another boy. The room was loud and full of smoke. The dancers clung to each other and staggered about the room. Sam went outside and found a vacant spot on the porch. He sat, and rolled a cigarette. He did not particularly care for Christmas. He missed Kate, and he thought of the time he and Mutt and Gus had enjoyed the little candles, and it was warm and safe and he had gotten a pocket knife. He missed them, too. Sam walked out to the pasture. It was quiet there, and the sky had cleared and the stars shone so, that it seemed like they were only a few feet away. He took a long drag on his cigarette and threw it away. He watched the steam of his exhaled breath and smoke drift across the pasture, illumined by the starlight. Kate had gone back to Illinois. Her letters had become fewer until there were none. Then, one day she wrote to tell him that she was going to marry a man and move to Chicago. He was a doctor, and she worked as his nurse. It was for the best, she said. He had never replied. Sam had stayed at Mr. Harris's house on the creek, and Ed continued to work the land and make liquor. Ed's enterprise had become sizeable, with customers in surrounding counties as well as in Hamilton. He paid Sam good money to deliver the whiskey, and had bought him the Ford for the purpose.

The party concluded just before sunrise. Much liquor was consumed; the splinters were danced out of the floor and the fist fights were finished. Sam had partaken of little liquor and less dancing. He had not intended to stay the night, but decided to stick around to help Ed home. He sat on the bumper of his car and watched the sky redden to the east. Christmas morning dawned, bitter-cold and clear.

CHAPTER 2

Sam sat on the porch of the house on Pecan Creek and watched the shadow creep from west to east across the yard as the sun set. The trees stood black against the late winter sky, but the tops still held some of the gold of the fading light. It was a Saturday at the end of February, and though he had been expected at Ed's, Mr. Harris had held him at the shop to do inventory. Sam didn't mind. At the shop, he imagined his circumstances were better. He wore a waistcoat and a tie, and his clothes were clean, and the store was warm, and his employer kind. Ed would have to wait.

He had taken to attending a little church in town when he could. It was an old Episcopal church full of mostly old Episcopalians. When Ed inquired, Sam said it was the only place in town he could get a drink on Sunday morning. Ed had laughed, but Sam was somewhat serious about his churchliness. He liked to take communion, and in fact, the blood of Christ was still a sweet wine, and its use was tolerated by local authorities. A Baptist had approached Sam about getting whiskey for a relative with pneumonia. The congregant felt sure that an Episcopalian such as Sam would be able to obtain it. Sam inquired of Ed for a donation. He agreed, and after some rummaging around, found a jar of some particularly foul shine and handed it to Sam.

"Ed, you really wanna give 'em this awful stuff?"

Ed grinned. "S'good enough for them Prohibitioners." On Sunday morning, he decided to attend church before meeting Ed. Sunday afternoons were his time to make deliveries, and he thought Ed could wait a bit longer. Sam left town after church, and after adjusting and readjusting the spark on the Ford many times it finally sputtered to life. It was midafternoon by the time he left town. Ed would not be pleased.

The afternoon was clear, and the warmth of late had begun to stir the soil. Sam could smell the ground waking up and breathed it in with big gulps. He made the top of the first river terrace when he saw smoke coming from the valley. He feared the still had exploded. By the time he had descended the second, he could see that the cabin was burning. By the time he descended the last terrace, Sam saw Ed lying in the yard. He pulled the Ford into the door yard, and killed the engine. The silence was so harsh, it astonished him. He could not move. The only sound was the sparks popping in the smoldering pile. Ed lay on his back. His mask was gone. Judging from the condition of his chest and head and the number of hoof prints around, he had been trampled to death. The contents of the cabin were strewn about the yard. Sam found a blanket and wrapped Ed in it. He dragged him to the passenger seat of the car and bound him upright with wire. The trip to town was long, and he had to tie Ed upright again before he reached the doctor. Sam talked to Ed. Through his tears, he apologized for being late; he thanked him for being his friend; he asked him not to die.

He took Ed to a doctor in Hamilton, but it was clear that Ed had died many hours ago and probably the night before. Sam made arrangements for his burial, and returned to the cabin. Only one wall remained standing. The fire had caught the long grasses around the house and several acres still smoldered. The still had been beaten into a mass of misshapen copper. Sam's grief was dwarfed by his rage. He looked for Ed's shotgun, and found it in the trampled grass where his body had lain. The Sheriff arrived before Sam could leave.

"I should have put an end to this when I first heard of it," he said. "It's obvious some rival distiller got rid of his competition. You know who did this, Sam?" Sam shook his head. He told the Sheriff that everybody liked Ed, and though he made moonshine, he was otherwise honest. The Sheriff looked Sam over, and asked him of his whereabouts the night before. Though the questioning was perfunctory, he told Sam to stick around town in case other questions needed answers.

Sam arrived at the gate of the Winkler place not long before sunset. He parked the car near the gate, but hid it within the thicket along the fencerow. The river made the west boundary of the land. A wooden bridge spanned the river through the dense trees. He waited. Winkler's house sat a hundred yards beyond, at the edge of the woods along the Leon bottoms. In the shadow he could see lights begin to glow from a window, then two. Smoke began to curl from the chimney. He assumed that Puddy still sponged off of his uncle, and would at least show up for meals. Just after sunset, Sam heard hoof beats coming up the road in the opposite direction from which he had come. They echoed on the wooden planks of the bridge and grew louder as he approached. Sam slammed a shell in the shotgun and slid from his seat. He crouched behind the fender and watched Puddy emerge from the dark of the woods on a pus-colored mare. When Puddy was within a few yards of the car, Sam stepped into the road. "Get down, Puddy Baker," he choked through clenched teeth. Puddy whirled the horse to flee. Sam fired, and Puddy dropped from the saddle. His body was a dark lump in the road ditch. Sam pulled the empty and reloaded. He approached Puddy, and poked him with the barrel of the shotgun. Puddy's right leg was a mass of blood and bone splinters, but he was alive. Winkler had arrived and hollered from the gate, but Sam didn't answer. Puddy, however, screamed in pain and called to his uncle, who now slowly approached Sam.

"Don't shoot, whoever you are." Winkler shouted.

Sam identified himself. "This son of a bitch killed Ed Wright, and I'm either gonna kill him here in this ditch, or take him to the Sheriff. It's your choice Mr. Winkler."

Winkler scratched the whiskers on his neck and knelt next to Puddy. "True what he said? Did you kill that Wright boy?" Puddy didn't answer but moaned that he would get even with Sam if it was the last thing he did on this earth. Sam jammed the barrel of the gun into one of the holes in Puddy's leg.

"Answer the goddamned question you piece of shit!" he hissed. Puddy threatened and whined and moaned and then soiled himself. Sam hit him in the face with the butt of the gun. Winkler reached for the shotgun, but Sam leveled it on him. "Stand back Mr. Winkler." he said. "He's gonna tell you, or I am gonna kill him where he lays." Sam pressed the barrel of the gun against Puddy's head and leaned on the butt.

"Awright! Awright! Me and some other boys run him down. We just wanted to hurt him! Just hurt him!!"

Winkler and Sam wrapped Puddy's leg and shoved him into the seat of the car. Winkler squeezed in next to him and said grimly, "I'm goin' with ya to make sure you don't kill him on the way, and to tell the Sheriff what I heard." He took off his hat and rubbed his face with both hands. "If this don't beat all." he said. "If this don't beat all."

CHAPTER 3

The trial took most of June before a hung jury set Puddy loose. He never disclosed the identity of those who rode with him, and some believed that one or two jurors had been part of the gang that night. For a man of so few admirable qualities, Puddy Baker had a sizeable following in town. Sam ignored most of the talk, and never attended the trial. He was aware of the precarious situation he was now in and carried Ed's shotgun and a cheap little pistol which held four bullets. He hoped for the best, and was determined to continue his efforts to establish himself. Ed's death had left him in sole possession of the land and its ruined improvements. He visited weekly, and sat on the stoop of the burned out cabin. On a hot July morning, he watched heat waves shimmer across the fallow corn field. Beyond the corn, bur oaks and a few water oaks grew along a little creek which joined the river. Though he tried to force his mind toward the promise of merchantable timber, and feed corn and corn liquor, he failed. The land was the place where he had lost both Kate and Ed, and would forever remain so. He had written Kate regarding Ed's death, but the letter had not been answered.

Sam walked to the hiding place for the still. It was in a little forested cove which ran perpendicular to the river. The canopy of trees made a cool shady spot to rest, and he leaned his back against an old hackberry. Someone had scavenged the copper shortly after the killing. It made little difference to Sam, who now eyed the ruins. A little pyramid of rocks at the base of a red oak caught his eye. He wondered if Ed had built it. He had taken away the top two stones when he saw the top of the cash box buried beneath. He pulled it out and blew the dirt away from the little padlock which held it closed. He pried at it with his pocket knife, but resorted to smashing it with a stone. It fell open. Paper money and coins fell out on the dirt and leaf litter at Sam's feet. It was almost two thousand dollars. Sam had no idea that Ed had prospered so much and was dismayed that he had shared so little.

Sam deposited the money in the bank, and resumed a life which no longer pleased him. He lived in the Harris's house on the creek, and continued work as a salesman. Without Ed, there seemed to be little to look forward to. Sam considered going back to the woods and hunting for a living. However, it seemed more level-headed to find some land and start a stock farm. Most of the bottomland had been bought up and put in cotton, but the thin soiled uplands were only good for cattle. Sam thought that he might be able to buy a little hard scrabble country cheap, and have a place where he could scratch out a living, and be in the brush and woods when he needed to be.

On a Saturday, he treated himself to lunch at a café which occupied the site of the once-renowned Watson saloon. The bar and the bottles were gone, but the fine tables and spittoons were the same. Mr. Winkler sat in a corner by a dusty window and was applying a fair amount of soup to his shirt front. His whiskers diverted most of the flow from his mouth. He motioned to Sam to join him. Sam pulled a chair to the table and sat.

"Howdy, Sam," said Winkler with a mouth full of corn bread. He held up his finger to pause the conversation long enough to swallow his bite. "I wanted to let you know that Puddy has left for Oklahoma to work in the oil fields there, such as the Sheriff suggested," he said. "You won't have to be looking over your shoulder quite as much, but I will tell you this: Puddy don't give up. If he comes back twenty year from now, he will be lookin' to even things up. If I am still around at that time, I will warn ya." Sam thanked Mr. Winkler. "And another thing" Winkler said, "I don't think you are gonna have much use for that forty acres. I figure I could buy it from ya. Think about it and how much you want for it, and let me know." Sam agreed to think about it

Sam wanted enough land to run some cattle. He didn't want the land on the Leon, but wanted a spread big enough for cattle, a section or more eventually, but less would do for now. About a week after his conversation with Winkler, a public notice appeared in the newspaper. Ruder Bilch had died in debt, and his heirs were breaking up the ranch. Bilch's heirs were distant cousins from Alabama and Georgia. They did not appear to have any interest in taking up a life in Texas. Sam solicited and received a week's leave from work; packed up a few belongings and tied them to a rented mule. He would stake his claim on Bilch's land.

He paid fifty dollars earnest money, and received a chit and a sack of stakes from Bilch's attorney that identified him as an honest bidder. He then took the same route he and Gus had taken on the trip to Fairy. The gate was tied tight, but the wire was not twisted with the same ferocity as it had been the day he and Gus and ridden through. The range northeast of town was green and lush. The cattle had been sold off and the land had been rested for more than a year. Almost every tall weed supported a small yellow and brown bird which sang at the top of its lungs. There were thousands. So many, Sam thought, that he could not hear himself think.

A few hundred acres of good grass would have made a good start, but Sam could see much of the level and rolling land had been claimed. It would be expensive as well. He decided to push up into the hills away from the Fairy road. There was a plateau northwest of the level ground. It was dissected by numerous narrow canyons that drained to the level lands south. The white chalk stood out against the black backdrop of a storm moving in from the northwest. Sam watched its progress until he determined that it would not hit until after sunset, so he continued. He dismounted and climbed into one of the larger of the little canyons. Its walls were sheer limestone, but the floor of the canyon had thick tall grasses and scattered cottonwood trees. Sam began to think that capturing water might be as important as buying thick grass. After he ascended the plateau, he rode along the heads of the canyons. Several had cottonwood, but most had little red oaks and ash and skunkbrush. They looked dry. The flats of the plateau had a reasonable amount of soil, Sam judged, and the grasses were short —types he had heard Gus call mesquite and buffalo grasses. The canyons and plateau would not support many cows, but sheep and goats would probably thrive on it.

Sam continued north until he came to some oak groves. Three live oak mottes grew next to a little creek. The creek still flowed, which impressed Sam, given that it was well into summer. He pulled his mule into one of the mottes and hobbled him; collected some firewood and prepared for the storm, which came at sunset and with such ferocity that Sam was afraid the mule would break its hobbles A ball lightning

170

moved through the adjacent clump of live oaks. He could hear it spit and sizzle as it rolled through the woods. The trunks of the trees and the underside of the canopy were lit by strong blue light. The ball bounced twice as it exited the motte, and then disappeared. Sam had heard of such lightning and St Elmo's fire as well, but had seen neither. The ball lightning unnerved him. He had been alone at night in the brush and prairies many times, but the night was strange. The intensity of the storm slowly diminished, but sheet lightning kept the inside of the motte illumined. Sam saw someone standing in the clearing just beyond the trees. The figure paced a little and jiggled coins in his pocket. Sam called out, but the figure did not reply. He found his cheap little pistol in his vest pocket, checked that it was loaded and ventured into the clearing. The figure had not moved. As he approached, the man turned to Sam, and he could see that it wore Ed's mask. "Ed?" Sam whispered. The man raised his hand as if to keep Sam at a distance. Then he disappeared. Sam sat down hard on the soggy ground.

Sam kept vigil most of the night and in the morning, he had decided that Ed had paid him a visit; that Ed approved of the spot, and that Ed wanted to be reinterred there. All of this satisfied Sam, and made the visit benign and possibly even a boon. After Ed's visit, Sam talked to him constantly. As he staked out what he thought would be close to 500 acres, he described his plans, how much the land would cost, how many goats he could run. He talked to Ed all the way back to Hamilton where he met the real estate man. The land Sam had selected was so poor that Sam was able to acquire it for five dollars an acre. The real estate man laughed when Sam drew the tract on the map.

"A cow would have to have a mouth as wide as a gate, and graze at a gallop all day long to survive on that land, son," the real estate man chuckled. Sam did not reply, but paid for the purchase of four hundred fifty acres of sorry land. The rest he held to fund improvements. He contacted Mr. Winkler and within a week had sold Ed's and his tract for a thousand dollars and was negotiating for fencing material the next day. Sam continued to work for the Harris's a few more weeks. They had been good to him, and he felt guilty about leaving. However, they encouraged him to move on, and gave him a fifty-dollar bonus and a nice cake for his time of service.

The first order of business was to fence the tract. The steep bluffs supported two types of cedar, the red cedar making the best fence posts. Sam found a crew of Mexican post cutters. They were small wiry men who never seemed to fatigue and worked for little money. It was August, and the heat was so fierce that Sam and his crew agreed to hide in the shade of a ledge of limestone until the heat broke. The men usually wore hats pulled down low over their brows, making it hard to determine features. Out of the sun, the men removed their hats, though some lay down and placed them over their faces. Sam studied the lines of the face of the man who sat next to him. He came slowly to the realization that the man had been one of the Villistas who had been his captor or caregiver in the little adobe house.

Sam smiled at him and asked, "Villista?" The man looked startled and said in English,

"No, I was not one of the General's men."

Sam grinned. "But you *were* one of those who kept me, a soldier, in the little adobe house." Sam laughed and almost

172

rolled off his seat. "It's not a problem, señor; it is just a very small world, as they say! Just too many beans, there, but I like those Mexican cigarettes!"

The man, whose name was Domingo, laughed, threw his hat on the ground and poked his finger at Sam. "I remember you! You did enjoy the visit!"

"What became of Dr. Najera?" asked Sam.

"In the government. He will be president someday." said Domingo. He smiled and shook Sam's hand.

Over the next few weeks they cut almost enough cedar to provide posts for all of the perimeters. Sam considered the pasture too rocky and brushy for cattle and had found enough Angora goats to start a herd. The next step was to cut thousands of smaller wire posts which would tie into the wire and keep the goats. "A goat is an animal looking for a way out," said Domingo, "but these should keep them in for a while, if you are good at mending fence." Sam laughed. The crew brought its food, mostly beans, but on the last night, Sam procured a kid goat and the crew dressed it; buried it in a pit, and built a fire over it. They sat under the ledge and drank Domingo's tequila and a bit of Sam's moonshine. The next morning, they unearthed the goat and spent the remainder of the day eating and sleeping. The next day, they packed their gear and were gone.

In their absence, Sam could hear his heartbeat in his ears. The quiet was deafening. The goats, to be shipped by train, had not arrived and there was little to do but wait. He had found a little cave about 10 feet deep, in which he laid cedar bows to make a bed. The weather had turned humid and hot, and the cave was the only cool place to take shelter. He lay on the bed for a day. He missed Gus and Charlie. He missed Kate. But most of all he missed Ed. The longing turned into a sadness he could not explain. It was hard to crawl out of the cave. Sam decided that he would pack some food and explore his land. Early the next morning, he climbed the highest bluff, and sat. The sun had not yet broken the horizon. Fog lay in the coves and bends around the hill, giving him the feeling he was sitting on top of the clouds. The air smelled wet and full of cedar sap. The slope below him had been cut for posts, and the sap was drying on the stumps. The sun came up under a deck of clouds and the land turned red in an instant. Sam walked first to the gate. He peed on the fence post and laughed. "Like a dang dog." he chuckled. From the gate he could see a long way south across the former Bilch range. The grass was high and full of dew.

He followed a ridge that ran north. To the east the bottomland along the creek was lush with grass. Little islands of ten to fifteen acres had grass as high as his waist, but there was not enough to support more than a few cows. That would have to come later after he got more land. At the north boundary, he could see the grassy valley running to the forest along the river. He was not far from where Bilch's cowboys had beaten him. He picked up a rock, cursed and threw it in that direction.

CHAPTER 4

By fall, Sam had dredged out two little ponds on the creek and had built a holding pen for his stock, which had finally arrived: ten Angora does and two bucks of which he was quite proud. He trained them to come to him by offering a little feed. Varmints were abundant in the hills, and Sam brought his stock in each night. He enclosed the front of the cave with rock and cedar posts, though he still cooked outside. His diet was mostly coffee and tinned meat, so fire was usually only required to boil coffee. He had gotten a used cook stove over which he fashioned a canvas tarp to keep out the rain and bird droppings. He had no neighbors, yet, and was the first to improve his property. Sam still had the little Ford, but rarely went to town. Once a month was sufficient to keep him supplied with potted meat, coffee, and the few building materials needed.

Sam had decided that Ed's relocation would have to wait. Instead, he built a monument out of limestone, which would do until he had enough money to pay for his re-interment. He carved Ed's name and death date on the hardest and flattest rock he could find. He did not know Ed's birthday. When he finished Ed's, Sam thought it would be fitting to carve one each for Charlie and Gus. By the following spring he had added tombstones for his mother and sister. He later added two more for Oscar and Kate, though of course she was not dead, but just as gone. A little cemetery surrounded Sam's shack. In the mornings, he took his coffee there and thought of the many he had lost, and otherwise admired his handy work. His does had eight kids, seven of which had survived. The eighth had disappeared, and Sam found a tuft of goat hair on the north fence. Likely a bobcat had carried him off into the woods. He had no resentment. Varmints had to eat, too, but he thought it might be wise to dispatch the cat. The goats were sheared by another Mexican crew, and Sam was paid enough to buy a few more goats.

The spring browse was good, and shrubs that had been goat-nipped sprouted vigorously with tender leaves and stems. The goats were getting fat after a lean winter. Sam was working on piping a spring when he saw the Sheriff pull up at the distant gate. As the car moved up the field lane, he could see that Mr. Winkler was with him. They stopped short of Sam's camp and walked in. "Sam? How is the life of the goat herd? Like it better than shop keeper?" the Sheriff smiled. Sam laughed and said it was hard work but the company was worth it.

Winkler sucked his teeth, kicked at a stone and said, "I told you I would let you know if Puddy came around. He was at my door last night, but I turned him away. We thought you should know, Sam. Just keep an eye out. He may have come back to settle a score with you. His leg ain't been much use since your little party."

The Sheriff nodded to Sam's little cemetery. "Who's buried in there?" Sam explained that they were just monuments to people he had lost.

My lord, and you so young." said Winkler. The Sheriff and Winkler exchanged a few pleasantries then left. The news was not good. He had a single shot shotgun and the little revolver. Not enough if Puddy came with company.

After several weeks, Sam decided Puddy had moved on. He finished piping the spring to his camp, so he would not have to haul water for his coffee in the morning. He built a trough for the goat pen and built a sluice to fill it. Rain became more frequent, and the goats got fatter accordingly. His camp had become a comfortable home. For the first time since Ed's death, it seemed to Sam that God was once again in His heaven.

On an early Saturday morning, Sam went to Hamilton to buy his coffee and tins of meat. The streets were crowded by cars and trucks now, and not the horses and buggies of his childhood. The early morning light made the courthouse shine like the moon. He caught his reflection in a pane of glass and marveled at how long his hair was. It occurred to him that he had no mirror and had become unaware of his appearance. He stepped into a barbershop which was full of old men and wiggly young boys getting their monthly haircuts. The air was full of cigarette smoke and ozone. As he waited for a chair to open, Puddy Baker peered in the window. His nose made a greasy spot on the glass. His eyes roved blindly over the crowd until he saw Sam. Their eyes met. Puddy made a grin that looked like a snarl, and he walked on. Sam did not wait for his haircut, but made his way out the back door into the alley. He entered the hardware store from the back door and purchased a Winchester lever action rifle and a box of bullets. He loaded the rifle and returned to the street. Puddy was gone, and Sam decided to postpone his shopping. He found his car and drove back to the farm.

The days were blazing, but the heat broke by late afternoon. Nights were dry and cool. Sam had taken to sleeping in his little cemetery. If Puddy showed up, he would be trapped in the cave. The tombstones would give him some cover if it came to a fight. He slept out for a week, and when Puddy didn't arrive, he again assumed that Puddy had, perhaps, moved on. However, the nights were pleasant, and Sam still made his bed in the cemetery. Though no moon shown, the star light illuminated the ground. He had been asleep for a few hours, when he woke to a shadow moving between the goat pens and his shack. It was a man, and he appeared to carry a shotgun. Sam had slept with his rifle. The figure entered the shack and the night erupted with a shotgun blast. The flash of the muzzle in the little room was so bright it took some time for Puddy's eyes to adjust. He stumbled out of the door and fumbled with the gun. Sam called out, "Puddy Baker!" Puddy stopped, chambered another shell, and brought the butt of the gun to his shoulder. Sam pulled his trigger and Puddy fell.

Sam stepped cautiously to the prone figure. Puddy Baker lay on his back. His mouth was open and he stared at the sky. The shot had hit Puddy squarely in the middle of his chest. Sam prodded him with the barrel of the rifle, and then felt for breath. He was dead. Sam's ears were still ringing and a pall of smoke hung over the camp when he dug a grave at Ed's marker. "Well, Ed, that should suit the most discriminating." he said as he covered the mound with leaves and rocks. He considered going for the Sheriff, but figured he was owed his killing. When he saw Mr. Winkler he would tell him that he had not seen Puddy. Maybe Winkler would be just as happy to be rid of him, he thought.

CHAPTER 5

In early August, he decided to find the bobcat. He had found scat along the north boundary of the property as well as a few tufts of hair the cat had left climbing the barbed wire. Sam put the stock in the pen and left enough food and water to carry them for two days. He thought it better than leaving them on the range for coyotes to eat, but if the cat got into the pen, it would be a slaughter. He packed the shotgun and a bit of food and walked the ridge north. The day was dawning hot. By the time he reached the north fence, his clothes were sweated through. He looked across the fence to the grassy valley and woods beyond. Sam felt a bit of trepidation as he hoisted himself into the terrain that had hosted his downfall years before. However, the grass was lush and high, and he remembered that Gus had told him that much of the land looked like this in the old days. When the wind caught the grass; it flashed silver and shined. Bilch had managed the land well despite his other failings. The grass was wet, though, and by the time Sam made the edge of the woods, his pants were soaked. He knew he would have a bumper crop of chiggers by the time he camped that night.

Sam skirted the edge of the woods looking for sign. He soon came upon a game trail which burrowed through a thicket of greenbrier and into the woods. The trail was clear on the other side, and soon he was in open woods. Bur oaks and hackberry towered over an open forest floor. Sam knelt and looked for tracks. Most of the tracks were coyote and raccoon, but in a muddy spot, Sam found cat tracks. They were fresh, and were headed into the deep woods. He thought it would be best to find a place near the trail and hope that

179

the bobcat would come back this way to visit his goat pasture. He stepped a hundred yards off of the trail, where he found white sage. Sam stripped, and smeared sage over his body. The morning's sweat gave him a loud odor, which would not do for tracking a wary cat. He took a small bundle and lit it with a Sulphur match. With this he smudged his clothes and gear. It was several hours before sunset, so Sam decided to nap. He was asleep with his mouth open when a leaf- footed bug landed in it. He woke with a start. The sun was low on the horizon. He repositioned himself and sat in the brush nearer the trail. The cat did not show up that night, or the morning of the next day. Disappointed, Sam followed the game trail further into the woods. The cat's tracks, a day or so older were clear. As he approached the river, he began to see more tracks. He initially thought they were the tracks of a man, but on closer examination, Sam saw clearly that they were bear tracks.

Happily, the cat had quit molesting the goats. Sam continued his work. The fence, as Domingo had predicted, was constantly challenged by the goats. They were especially talented at worming their way under the bottom strand. At the end of the summer, his thoughts began to linger on the bear tracks. He had been certain that Charlie had shot the last bear on the Leon. He did not have Charlie's knowledge, though and could not read the bear's age, gender or intentions from tracks. As the summer slipped away, he decided to look for the bear in the fall. There were stands of oaks, and he thought the bear could be found there when the acorns dropped. November rolled in with dark clouds and sleet. This would be the time the bear would be stuffing itself for the coming winter. He followed the ridge north again, but this time, the aspect of the woods was different. With most of the leaves gone, he could see a hundred yards or more into the forest. As he entered, the atmosphere changed. The wind dropped, though he could hear the clatter of the branches in the wind fifty feet above him. He looked through the bare branches to the sky, and could see that the sky had darkened even more. He had better find a place to camp for the night.

Sam was gathering wood when the snow began to fall. It was still warm enough that the snow fell in wet balls of slush. He made a good fire and built a lean-to. The following morning, the snow had accumulated in the trees, though it was spotty on the ground. A little bit of snow would help with the tracking. In the morning, it was cloudy and cold, but still. He picked up his rifle and stuffed some food in his pocket and walked toward the river. As he got closer, the canopy of the forest lifted, and most of the trees were oak. One of the trees had been marked by the bear. The bark was raked with claw marks. Sam looked at the tracks around the tree, which he thought were about two days old. They were filled with snow, but had no leaves or other debris in them. Sam walked in concentric circles around the tree until he found another set of newer tracks. These had been left in the snow, and led to a piece of roughed-up ground where the bear had uncovered acorns.

Sam smudged again and buried himself in the leaf litter as Charlie had shown him many years ago. Dusk was a few hours away, and he expected the bear to return. He slept. He dreamed of Charlie. In the dream, Charlie was a Comanche. He didn't really look like Charlie, but Sam knew it was him. Charlie had a long lance in his hands and was fighting a ferocious bear. The bear stood on his hind legs and roared and swiped at Charlie with enormous paws. He jabbed at the bear's underbelly with the lance. Suddenly, the bear and Charlie quit fighting. The bear sat down on its haunches, and Charlie turned, smiled at him, and said, "Some bears are just for admiring." Sam awoke as the sun set red in the west. He heard twigs and branches snapping. A very large, very old bear was standing, rubbing his back on a tree. He appeared to be twice as large at the shoulders as at the hips. His face was wide and scarred. His belly hung almost to the ground, and he was swaybacked. The bear turned as he dropped on all fours. In his exposed side Sam saw a perfectly round bare spot in his fur, a gray scar the size of the slug Charlie had fired at a young boar fifteen years before. Sam was astonished at the coincidence. Could this be the bear that Charlie had presumably killed just before Bilch's cowhands killed him? The cowboys had not lingered to claim the bear, and had dragged Charlie's body and Sam away. Perhaps the bear had survived and gone on its way. Perhaps this was the ghost of the bear, though he didn't think a bear killed in its youth would have a ghost so big and old. The bear was oblivious to Sam. Sam watched in fascination as the bear fed on acorns. The bear then sat and Sam lay nearby, and they watched the evening draw into night together.

BOOK 4

CHAPTER 1

The crash of 1929 took everyone by surprise, though Texans seemed to believe it would not affect them. By the mid 1930's Texans believed it. Cash was short, rain was sparse, and weeds grew in the yards of many of the fine old houses in Hamilton. The price of mohair dropped by half. Sam was an exception in having no debt and half his former income. By local standards, he was almost rich. The tracts around Sam were abandoned. Some had never been improved by the new owners, and the grass was rank. Sam was able to purchase from his neighbors over two sections at pennies on the dollar and had acquired others for near nothing on the courthouse steps. It saddened him that his neighbors had fallen on hard times, and that he was the beneficiary. However, it had been hard times which had allowed the elder Bilch to assemble the ranch in the 1880's.

He bought a little under a hundred head of white face cattle and stocked the range. Each animal would have about thirty acres to graze per year. He wanted the tall grass to persist. A neighbor had made it through the hard time by moving in two hundred head of horses on his two sections. Drought, while bad in Hamilton County, had been worse west and north. Several in the County had taken on horses from drought stricken horse farms in the plains. Sam had watched as the tall prairie grasses were replaced by buffalograss, broomweed and prickly pear. Gus had shown him the land as it was in the old days. Sam intended to keep his part intact if he could. But in the third year of drought the range was depleted. Tallgrasses were scattered, and weeds and short grasses grew between the clumps. Despite the continuous browsing by the goats, brush had increased on the rocky pastures. Bare ground, which was once only common in the limestone hills, appeared on the deeper soil as well. Sam found one of his young bulls dead on a rocky knoll not far from the little house he had built before the bottom fell out of the country. The carcass had been chewed by the coyotes, and had decayed to the extent that only the backbone, ribs, skull and a little hide were left. A bower of lush grass grew around the bull. The grass stems mimicked the barrel of the ribs. It was hard to tell where grass ended and the bull began. Sam lay on his belly and looked through the tunnel of ribs, which framed the sunset. He wondered what kind of bower his body would make if he were left in peace on that little knoll. The cows lost weight, and the continued drought and lack of forage made them vulnerable to disease. He sold off the cattle, but kept the goats, who appeared resistant to the drought. Trees died, but the brush and shrubs the goats relished grew where the grass and trees failed.

Dust storms from the high plains rolled in with regularity. Though they were deadly up on the High Plains, they were more a nuisance in central Texas. They had the same effect on him as did thunderstorms. He climbed the knoll to watch their approach with anticipation; watched the distant land being swallowed by them. The silence they brought was as intense as thunder. When they came he felt insulated, protected. He sat inside the cave when they came, the air being a little better there. They were sometimes followed by muddy raindrops as big as silver dollars, which stuck to the few living things on the range and choked them.

The cattle tanks had dried up, but the spring flowed, though less vigorously than in the past. The goats came to drink twice a day and that is when he discovered five missing. Sam picked up his rifle and walked the fence line to detect the passage of any varmints. As the depression had progressed, most edible animals in the neighborhood had been hunted to near extinction. He had not seen a raccoon or a possum in a year, though he doubted people had turned to coyotes or bobcats for sustenance. One morning, Sam saw smoke rising from the river bottoms. He found a camp of about fifteen people. There were women and children. He climbed the fence and walked cautiously into the camp. It was silent, and the adults looked at him with pinched faces and narrowed eyes. The children had the same suspicious look, but averted their eyes. Their clothes were worn out and their cars and the few tents had seen hard use. Sam hollered, "Those goats are all I got. I ain't going to get the Sheriff, but you leave the goats alone, you hear?" Three of the men approached Sam, and he chambered a shell in the rifle. They stopped.

The oldest stepped forward and said, "We don't aim to cause you any trouble mister. We just have children to feed. Do you have any work for us to do?" Sam replied that he did, but he had little money to pay. The old man spat on the ground and walked away. "We'll be outa here by morning." Sam had a nuisance buck, which was the ring leader for animals getting out. He always found the weak spot in the fence. He had castrated it the spring before, but old habits die hard. In the evening, he tethered the goat to the fence. In the morning it was gone.

CHAPTER 2

Ten days after Pearl Harbor, Sam learned of the attack and declaration of war. The clerk in Hamilton's hardware store informed Sam and looked at him like he had just fallen out of the sky. Sam was shocked by the declaration of war, and even more so that he was more than a week late learning about it. He explained that mail came once a week; he had no electricity to run a radio, and his visitors were infrequent. The clerk looked down his nose at him. Sam purchased a radio at great expense and, on his way home, saw a junked flatbed truck on the side of the road. Abandoned cars were common, their being so many fleeing the region in cars little better than junk to begin with. He lifted the hood, fought off a flurry of red wasps, and detached the generator. He spun it a few times, and the lack of grinding satisfied him that it might be serviceable. When he got home, he fashioned a whirligig from meat tins and attached it to the rotor of the generator. Once he had mounted it on the hill above his house, he wired it to the radio. The radio squawked and squealed. Finally, he found a station in Fort Worth. It was a broadcast concerning selective service and encouraging men to volunteer before their notices arrived. This was followed by an advertisement for lard, and then the farm report. The former and the latter caught Sam's attention. Though he was pushing forty, he might be expected to serve. More importantly, the wool market had made a huge jump, and was considered essential for the war effort. Uniforms were needed, and needed quickly. Sam arranged a farmer's deferment from the draft board, and bought as many hair goats as he could. He mortgaged a portion of his land and built more pens and a shed, and installed two windmills.

Sam was apprehensive that he had bitten off more than he could chew. Nineteen forty-one and early forty-two were dry years. The second shearing yielded only half of that of the spring. However, by the following summer, rain and browse were abundant. He was able to pay off the mortgage by his third year of expansion. He added rooms on the little house he had built. He stocked a few cows, and bought a pickup truck. He hired hands for fence work. He had never known such prosperity. He decided it was time to look for a wife.

CHAPTER 3

Though he was not enthused about the prospect of attending church, it appeared that it would be the most likely place to meet marriageable women. On his first Sunday, he spent an hour combing and re-combing his hair. He changed the part from the left to the right and back again. He had not studied his reflection in many years. He looked in a little mirror and evaluated his salability. His eyebrows stuck out like antennae on a bug. Wind and sun had wrinkled his face and hands to the extent he looked like an older man. Half of his fingernails were worn off from fence work and pulling rocks. He smelled like tobacco, goat and wood smoke, and he had no idea how to dress. He put on a clean white shirt and his cleanest pair of pants. He tucked them into his boot tops to hide the wear on his cuffs, donned his Stetson, and went to church.

The little white church on the outskirts of town was farther than he remembered. He was late, and in such a state of distracted anxiety that he slammed his fingers in the truck door. "Godamnit!!!" he hollered, realizing too late that the windows of the church were open. He lingered by the church door hoping that if enough time elapsed, he would not be identified as the person spewing profanity. He even paused to look disdainfully over his shoulder as he entered. Eventually, he found a seat on the last pew. The choir was singing "Nearer my God to Thee" and was made up of old women with warbly voices. It sounded like a whole room full of Mutts singing.

The congregation was made up of a few older men, but mostly women of various ages. The younger men were in the service; gone to war. Unfortunately, sitting as he was in the back of the church, he could only see hats and shoulders. Some of the shoulders had babies peering over them. One in the pew in front of him slobbered on his mamma's collar and stared balefully at him until, uncomfortable, Sam looked away.

The congregation met for coffee following the service. The pastor greeted Sam, who, being unpracticed at conversation, could only smile and nod. The pastor was a short man with a bald head. He stood too close and looked up Sam's nose. Sam shuffled his feet and stared at the wall above the pastor's head or at the women as they delicately ate their cookies and sipped coffee. It occurred to him that if he had an opportunity to speak to a woman, that he would have nothing to say. He barely knew how to converse with another man, and Kate was the only woman he had really ever talked to. The pastor reached out and grasped Sam's arm which caused him to flinch and drop his coffee cup. Sam apologized and as he bent to pick up the cup's shattered remains he bumped heads with the pastor who was bending to do the same. Sam left discouraged, though he chuckled when he opened the door to the pickup truck. He wondered what the congregation must have thought.

He stopped at his mailbox on the way into the farm. He had neglected collecting mail on Saturday. He flung the few envelopes onto the passenger seat and put the truck in gear to drive to the house. He glanced at the mail. Familiar handwriting caught his attention. It was a letter from Kate.

BOOK 5

CHAPTER 1

She sat on her front door stoop and smoked. Kate had the dregs of a tumbler of bourbon in her hand, and she flicked ashes into it. It was late September and the trees had just begun to turn. All summer, it seemed the leaves had dripped with tallow, it was so lush. Even the air dripped with life. Now, there was emptiness and dust in the air. She had not returned to her job at the hospital since Frank's death. He had been too damned old for the army in her opinion, but he was a surgeon and needed for the effort. She had tried to talk him out of it, but he had insisted. The irony that he had been chief surgeon in a field hospital in Belgium after D-Day, and survived all the danger and horror only to drop dead of a heart attack within weeks of his return home was almost funny. She thought he would have laughed had he known the story. But he didn't.

She and Frank had lived together in a smallish town north of Chicago for almost fifteen years. Frank was older than her, and she had fallen in love with him soon after she became his nurse. He was handsome and had thick black hair, grey in the temples. The rumble of his deep voice made the china in the cabinet rattle. He was something of an orator, and often gave speeches to Kate at the dinner table. She teased him that he would have made a good preacher. Kate pulled his overcoat from the closet and held it to her face. The smells were shaving cream, and soap and one that was just him. For the first month after his death, she wept

191

into the coat. Sat with it and hugged it to her. She talked to the wall and cursed him for leaving her. She was grateful that she and Frank had had no children. They had lived for themselves, and now the urge to leave Chicago was strong. The winters there were too cold and bleak. She didn't look forward to spending the next one alone. She remembered the Texas heat, and the wild country and the wild times there. She had been young there, and there had been Sam. She hung Frank's coat in the closet, and closed the door. She opened a dresser drawer and rummaged through some boxes. She pulled an old one from under the pile. It had once contained gauze, but Kate had filled it with keepsakes from her time in Texas. She lit another cigarette and sat on the edge of the bed. It had been years since she looked through the contents of the box. There were postcards and faded Brownie photos of the nurses at the field hospital. There were letters. Most of them were from Sam, in his scratchy, juvenile hand. Most were only a few sentences and comically formal. Kate smiled and took a long thoughtful drag on her cigarette.

She rose and walked to her dresser. She touched her hair and examined her face. She was still pretty, though her eyes were not as round and dreamy. The years had been hard at times, but she had aged well. The time after the war had been hard. She drank, though she never lost her ability to function. If anything, she thought, the drink had made the smile lines, though she knew they were really just wrinkles. She smiled. She wondered what Sam looked like after almost thirty years. The return address was Hamilton. She decided to take a chance.

CHAPTER 2

Sam braked the truck to a sudden stop in the middle of the field lane. The wind was out of the south, and the dust overtook him, making him cough. He held the envelope and savored it. He opened it neatly with his clasp knife and gently pulled out the letter. It was on thin paper —the thickness of cigarette paper. The handwriting was unchanged: neat cursive with a backward slant; a woman's hand. He read. She was coming to Hamilton. She had a car and would drive. Sam felt a mixture of elation and panic. He had just that morning examined himself in the mirror and found his appearance lacking. His house was full of dirt daubers, and cobwebs hung from the ceiling. He had not thrown a single empty chili can away. It had been his main sustenance for years, and the empties were piled in a corner of the kitchen. He lived happily with mice and the occasional rat snake. The letter continued that she did not know when she would arrive, but that she expected to be there in late October or early November. She told him to watch for her. He would.

Sam's work was frenzied for the next month. He painted the house; he cleared debris from decades of living alone; he bought new clothes, and went to the barber twice. In the afternoons he sat on the porch and watched the road for a telltale dust plume. He sometimes stood by the gate with his new haircut and new clothes hoping she would arrive when he was at his best. He did so through the last week of October. The chores of the ranch had gone untended. He had bought fifty Herefords to rotate with his goats, and had failed to keep up with the rotation. The range suffered for it.

However, Sam feared that Kate would not be the woman she had been, or perhaps the woman he thought she had been. He had changed himself. He had become so unused to human companionship that he did not know what to do with it when it dropped in his lap. By the first week of November, he abandoned the new clothes and porch sitting and was in the process of moving cattle and mending fence the day Kate arrived. She was sitting in a rocking chair on the porch when he pulled up to the house. Her hair was black and tied in a ponytail with a red ribbon. She wore pants and a soft pink sweater lay across her shoulders. She looked familiar without being so. He wore two old pairs of pants to keep the barbs at bay, and his sweaty hair was disheveled under his hat. However, without as much as dusting off, Sam walked to the yard gate and stood. He was transfixed. He could only grin and stare. The woman he had carried in his heart for many years was now sitting in his favorite chair. Kate smiled but did not speak. They stayed this way, yards apart, until Kate covered her mouth, laughing, and walked up to the gate. "Do you want to come in, Sam?" she smiled. He opened the gate, and they embraced. Sam ran a handkerchief under his nose, and she smiled up into his face, appraising him.

"I can't tell you how good it is to see you." he said. "It has been a long time without you, but I managed." Kate said nothing. She studied Sam's eyes. He looked sad, though she knew he was glad to see her. His face was lined and sunburned, but his eyes were the same. She took his hand, and they walked to the porch where they sat and watched the shadows get long.

The next day, they walked the ridge north toward the Leon River. Sam had packed a little sack of crackers and tinned meat and some water. His favorite place to admire the landscape was the end of the ridge, which dropped steeply off into the woods along the Leon. Kate had not packed clothes for the country, and only had some leather pumps to hike in. Sam gave her a pair of his better boots, and it amused him to see her in her wool skirt and tall boots. They were too big, and she stumbled frequently on the rocks. It was mid-afternoon, and the sky had taken on a leaden cast, and the wind was from the north and chill. Kate told him about as much as she could remember about the past thirty years. The feature which stuck with him most was her account of working in a field hospital in the First World War. She didn't say it had changed her, but Sam thought that it had. There was a hardness to her that was foreign to him. It seemed foreign to her, too. There had once been sweetness about her when she was young. Her emotions had been easy to move, but now she was so self-possessed that Sam was not sure she really required his company. The war had been terrible. As she talked, she seemed to become vulnerable; the old memories were still fresh. Her hands clenched and unclenched as she spoke. However, before she indulged them, she lit a cigarette and exhaled a cloud of blue smoke and smiled. "How has it been for you, Sam? These long years."

Sam told her about his financial success, starting with his partnership with Ed, and through the wool bonanza of the Second World War. He was too aware that she was a sophisticate. She was a woman who lived in Chicago, drove a car, dressed well, and smoked expensive cigarettes. The details of ranching and wool shearing and castration and the general dirt and tedium of it were an embarrassment to him. He told her about Ed's murder and the apprehension of

Puddy Baker, but chose to keep his killing to himself. He was honest about his grief in losing Ed, though. "I didn't take losing Ed very good," he said. "There were nights I missed him so much, I saw him walkin' around on this hilltop. I wish you had come for the funeral, but I know Chicago is an awful long trip and you had your reasons."

She touched his arm and looked into his face. "I'm sorry for that, Sam. I got your letter. Frank wasn't comfortable with my coming here, and I should have written, though I don't know what I would have said."

Sam shifted his seat and pointed out "That was a long time ago, Kate. You needn't worry about it, though I did wonder." She held his face with both her hands and kissed him on the mouth. Sam grinned and looked at the ground.

CHAPTER 3

Over the next week, Sam and Kate talked about their time on the border; their aspirations met and unmet. Sam felt that he had exhausted his supply of experience and conversation, but Kate always had more to add. She had lived more. Sam felt cowed by her worldliness and experience. He just didn't have anything to left to say. Kate filled the silence with new stories: more about the war in France, her work as a surgical nurse, her late husband, Chicago and New York. By the second week, however, their conversations were spare. Sam talked about the weather, and Kate talked about clothes and going to town to get her hair permed.

One night, they sat by the fire and said little. Then Kate asked, suddenly, "Who did you expect I would be, Sam? I mean after all these years." Sam was uncomfortable with the question.

He said, "I don't know, Kate. I guess I thought you would be you." He paused and rolled a cigarette. After he lit it, he exhaled the smoke, and looked at her directly. "I used to see the whole world in you — in your eyes. I saw all of the things I wanted and all the things as I might ever want them to be. I guess both of us were just in the beginning of becoming who we really were. Now, I guess you are you, with or without me."

Kate smiled and reached for Sam's hand. "I think I wanted to take you to Illinois, and make a corn farmer out of you."

Sam cleared his throat. "Well. I like Texas and I like my goats." he mumbled. Kate laughed.

"Sam, I think we were a big fire, and big fires burn out quickly." she said.

Sam frowned and said, "Why did you come, Kate? Why didn't you just stay where you were?"

Kate looked at Sam and said, "I just thought I needed to see if I was that young thing that loved you ... I needed to see if you were still you. You are, you know." She looked away from Sam. "But I'm not."

December was particularly cold. It had dropped below freezing and had stayed there for two weeks. The windmill, and the piping from the spring had frozen and some of the pipes had burst. This kept Sam in the field for several days at a time, leaving Kate to sit by the stove and listen to the live oak pop and hiss as it burned, and the wind hoot in the eaves as it found its way into the house. Sam assumed the fifteen years' accumulation of National Geographic magazine would keep her occupied. One afternoon, she ventured outside. She found Sam's old cave and the little cemetery. It was overgrown with the dead remains of the last summer's weeds, but she recognized the names. She had just found her own tombstone, when Sam returned from the pasture. He walked up behind her, and placed his hand on her shoulder. "This is just a memorial for all of those I lost." he said. "You weren't dead, of course, just lost." Kate pulled her coat up around her shoulders and said, "I'm not sure I want to be out here with the ghosts." She turned and walked back to the house.

Sam had spent the last month sleeping on a pallet in the room adjacent to the bedroom. He had given Kate his bed. He was close to sleep one night when he heard Kate weeping. He rose and tapped on the closed door. He entered. "What's wrong, Kate?" he whispered. She sobbed and reached for him. He lay on the bed and held her as she sobbed. He couldn't explain her sadness, though somehow he knew it. He knew that she had lost so much, and that he could not fill that emptiness. He knew, too, that time and distance and circumstance had changed too much between them. They were lost to each other.

CHAPTER 4

The wind blew hot from the southwest on Friday. The house was empty. The wind hissed through the shrub next to the porch, and rattled the window panes. He sat on the stoop and watched the dust blow up from the south pasture: the smell of dirt, the smell of exhausted soil. Two white tracks led south from the house to the county road. Heat waves rippled above them, though the day had barely begun. The tracks were the road out. The tracks were those she had taken to leave him. She had left in December, and it was well into June now. There was work to be done, but for now, it was sufficient to sit and watch the heat; to roll a cigarette and swat flies. She would not come again.

Today, he had awakened in the attic on a little cot he kept there. In the summers, the open windows and height kept a little breeze moving across him. In the coldest winters he moved downstairs to the bedroom where he could get the benefit of a nearby stove. This morning, the sun had just cleared the horizon when he stirred the ashes of the cook stove. He threw in a few chunks of live oak and fanned some lit newspaper beneath. He pulled on his boots and stumbled out to the chicken coop and collected three eggs. When he returned, he spat on the stove, and the sizzle told him it was sufficiently hot.

Sam sat on the old paint bucket next to the stove to drink his coffee. When he finished his eggs, he went to the windmill and flipped the lever to release the vane. Wind was sufficient to fill the cistern today, he thought. Besides, he liked the rhythmic chatter and clunk. It kept him company. It had been a month since he had rotated pastures. Too long in this dry weather and the land showed it. He usually paid attention to the needs of the cattle and the land, but it had been harder to stay on top of things since Kate had left. Today, he would move the stock to the bottom pasture, which had suffered less from the dry, and which he had held in reserve. It had once been a cotton field, and now rank Johnsongrass and scattered switchgrass grew. The cattle seemed eager to get to it, and Sam had to do nothing other than open the gate. It would hold them for a while, but he might have to sell off some stock to keep the herd numbers in balance with the droughty land.

He returned to the porch in the early afternoon. Around two, a thunderhead rose in the south and began to meander its way across the horizon. It came closer. He could see the distant blue shafts of rain. He could smell the soothing coolness, but it turned east before even the thunder could be heard. He loved her then and he loved her now. She would not come again.

Around the time the porch began to cast a little shade on the east side of the house, he stood and fumbled for the key in his pocket, and walked out to the truck. Because he used it to patrol his pastures, and rarely made it into town, he believed third gear shone clean and bright as the day it rolled off the assembly line. Sam drove the mile to the bluff, where he and Kate had watched the cold sky last fall. He backed the truck to the edge and killed the engine. He listened to the silence creep in. He liked to listen to the slow metallic click as the engine cooled. The truck bed had been his evening roost each day since she had left. At first he grieved for Kate, but after a few months he just remembered her; looked at pictures of her in his mind's eye. He liked to watch the hills on the far side of the river reflect the sunset. They were yellow, then red, then blue ... then gone. The stars came out. A little breeze rustled in the plums at the bottom of the bluff, climbed the slope, and touched his cheek before it moved to the oaks beyond.

Made in the USA
Lexington, KY
07 February 2018